These Prisoning Hills

ALSO BY CHRISTOPHER ROWE

Bittersweet Creek and Other Stories
Telling the Map

SUPERNORMAL SLEUTHING SERVICE
(with Gwenda Bond)
The Lost Legacy
The Sphinx's Secret

THESE
PRISONING
HILLS

CHRISTOPHER ROWE

A TOM DOHERTY ASSOCIATES BOOK

NEW YORK

THESE PRISONING HILLS

Copyright © 2022 by Christopher Rowe

Cover art by Sung Choi
Cover design by Christine Foltzer

Edited by Jonathan Strahan

A Tordotcom Book
Published by Tom Doherty Associates
120 Broadway
New York, NY 10271

www.tor.com

Tor® is a registered trademark of Macmillan Publishing Group, LLC.

ISBN 978-1-250-80449-5 (ebook)
ISBN 978-1-250-80448-8 (trade paperback)

First Edition: 2022

For Gwenda, who told me there was an empty car with an open door at the top of a hill

. . . I cannot go.

Being of these hills I cannot pass beyond.

—James Still

These Prisoning Hills

The human identities of the scholars and technicians who created, built, activated, and then were subsumed by the artificial intelligence that named itself Athena Parthenus remain unknown. We know their number, for it was they who became "the 36," the human components of the enormous Commodores. These beings evinced a complicated relationship with Athena. Who was the maker? Who was the made?

The frightfully powerful Commodores, above all the other mechano-nano-biological creatures who made up the military and governing apparatus of what became known as the Voluntary State of Tennessee, represented the greatest of Athena's threats to the federal and irregular forces arrayed against her. At the end of the first war, 28 of the 36 were discovered powered down in the ruins of Nashville. Seven, freed from the governance of Athena and operating at diminished capacity, were destroyed west of the Mississippi. One remained unaccounted for.

—*A History of the First Athena War*

NOW

Marcia tapped her temple. The state-provided eye she'd been fitted with when she'd been appointed county agent didn't penetrate the low gray clouds. She knew the federal lifter was up there somewhere—at least it was *scheduled* to be up there—but damned if she could make it out.

She'd been at the grange for an hour already, coaxing the little harvesters and their counterparts who worked the silos through the backbreaking labor of loading and unloading the gravity wagons with their steeply pitched beds. The gleanings of the hillsides were bound for coastal cities nobody in the county would ever see and few could even name. Some of the carefully tailored grain might even end up overseas, for all anyone in the county knew.

An indicator light floated in Marcia's vision, invisible to any onlookers. It began flashing amber.

After a moment, the lifter began descending through

the clouds, still concealed, but detectable by the swirls and eddies in the gray vapor.

The timing was good. The Federals were late, but they'd arrived before Marcia started thinking too much about the past. Thinking about the past—and about things that were concealed—crippled her some black nights.

The little harvesters scrambled clear of the grange's landing pad. Marcia rechecked the manifests, wondering if the lifter was empty—which would mean clearing out the silos and an attendant bonus credited to the county—or if it was late in its schedule of pickups—which might mean it couldn't take much of the harvest at all, leaving grain to rot.

There was a tug at her pants leg. One of the scar-faced silo hands, their skin tone an intense violet not found in nature like all the dependents of that specialty, looked up at her, blinking furiously and pointing out at the landing pad.

The lifter wasn't a lifter. An ugly black craft, bristling with sensor suites and weapons arrays, settled to the ground on jets of steam.

The little harvesters milled around in confusion.

Then one of them started hustling forward, pushing their gravity wagon. A couple of the smarter ones stopped them before they reached the pad.

The light in Marcia's field of vision had gone red. Her hands had gone cold.

"Agent, I don't need anything from you but a couple of updated maps and the name of a local willing to guide us back into the hills."

Marcia was sitting in the visitor's chair of her own small office. The captain, a jaundiced-looking Hispanic man wearing the same mottled brown and gray fatigues as the squad of federal soldiers he commanded, had taken the chair behind her desk without a word.

The federal military arriving unannounced wasn't something Marcia would ever have expected. But now that they were here, their commanding officer taking her chair without ceremony wasn't surprising. Marcia would have done the same once.

"As I already told your sergeant, the maps you have are the newest I've seen, certainly newer than anything we have here. Nobody goes to that part of the county—it's been quarantined since the peace. And we don't have the benefit of eyes in the sky."

The captain was probably thirty years younger than Marcia, too young to have fought in the war. But he had an edge to him. She didn't doubt his competence, just the wisdom of his requests. He nodded at her.

"We'll make do, then. What about a guide?"

He was ignoring what she'd said about eyes in the sky, which was probably a good thing for her. The high-flying drones and low-orbiting satellites the Federals used to monitor the Commonwealth and other treaty states were supposed to be secret because they were a violation of sovereignty. Marcia wasn't interested in an argument about sovereignty with a man in command of a gunship.

The captain was also ignoring what she'd said about nobody going to the uplands anymore.

"I don't have a name for you, Captain. The last census puts the county population at having dropped down to less than four hundred citizens, and maybe three times that harvesters, teamsters, and other dependents. I know them all. None of them know those hills."

The captain pulled a length of wire from a pocket. It glowed blue. He fed it into his temple.

"You know those hills, Agent," he said after a moment, his eyes distant and his voice hollow. "You were born in them."

She'd expected this as soon as the sergeant had let slip the broad outlines of their orders. She'd thought she was prepared for it.

"Captain, I am sixty-one years old. I left the uplands when I was sixteen. Since then, the whole range from the

Girding Wall north to . . . north to where I don't know, New England, maybe, have gone through the Reseeding. And here in the Commonwealth all the mountains were subjected to eight years of sustained bombardment by both your employers and by the Voluntary State."

The captain pulled the wire out of his temple. It was dull gray now. He dabbed at the blood that flowed down his cheek. "*Our* employers," he said.

"I'm not in service," Marcia said. "I went off active over twenty years ago and left the reserves five years after that. I'm not even in the county militia."

The captain shook his head. "I was referring to your current position."

"I'm an employee of the Commonwealth," she said, knowing he was going to have a reply she wouldn't like.

"The Homeland Consul placed this county under martial law the second we set down," he said. "All government functions have been assumed by the Consul. Local personnel will be kept in place for the duration of the crisis, of course. Where possible."

All Marcia knew about the supposed "crisis" was that it involved a platoon of federal troops marching into hills that had been unwelcoming to outsiders even before they'd been pulverized as a battleground by outside warring super-states, the Federals versus the Voluntary State of Tennessee. She thought she could hazard a guess about what was going on, though.

"There's something of hers up there," she said. "Some creature or piece of technology created by Athena Parthenus. Your spy eyes spotted it through the clouds and you're going after it."

The captain said, "Your records indicated that you're smart. But that's not quite it. Yes, there's someone or something active in the uplands connected to Athena Parthenus. Something now invisible to us. But we're not an extraction team. An extraction team has been on the ground for two weeks."

It clicked into place.

"You're the rescue team," said Marcia.

The records of the federal government concerning the Owls of the Bluegrass have yet to be declassified, leaving scholars to depend on anecdote, rumor, and even the apparatus of legendry that has grown up around the mysterious figures. Unlike their allies in the Crow Bands, the Owls closely guarded their true identities. Likewise, the source or sources of their uncanny cognitive abilities and comprehensive knowledge of the Voluntary State remain unknown.

—*A History of the First Athena War*

A LONG TIME AGO

Marcia was less surprised by the sight of the Owl creeping through the undergrowth toward her position on the firebase perimeter than she was by the fact that the helmeted woman had apparently not caught sight of *her* yet.

For while it was true that the camouflaged blind she and her seconds stood in high in the tree canopy was as well-concealed as the technology of the Expeditionary Force and the techniques of her forebears could make it, it was unheard of that an Owl of the Bluegrass be seen when they wished to be unseen, or to overlook any detail whatsoever, even concealed details.

A voice crackled in Marcia's earpiece. An unfamiliar voice.

"Captain, please have those in your charge refrain from firing upon me, or from otherwise impeding my progress."

Marcia cursed softly, rousing the corporal next to her, who had in point of fact been looking in entirely the wrong direction and thus had presented nothing in the way of a threat to the Owl in any case.

"Drop the ladder," she told the young man. "And radio in to the day officer that I'm bringing in a prisoner."

Her earpiece sounded again. The strange woman's strange voice echoed in Marcia's hearing. "A guest rather," she said. "Or better, a messenger."

The fact that the woman, in her helmet and feathered cloak, had compromised the base's communications was no real surprise. The fact that the Owl was unaccompanied, though, was unusual. Marcia had never encountered one of the cryptic mystics except in the company of a band of jeering and cawing Crows, members of the "independent soldiery" that had sprung up in the Commonwealth following the rise of the Voluntary State.

The designation Owls of the Bluegrass suggested that out in the wider world there were Hoosier Owls and Buckeye Owls and Owls of the Old Dominion, but Marcia was pretty sure there were no soldier savants dressed up as birds of prey in any of those places. Only here.

Here in general, in the Commonwealth of Kentucky, and here in particular, in the shadow of the run of the Girding Wall set hard against the foot of writhing, moaning Jellico Mountain, home to flora, fauna, and even geology corrupted by the incomprehensible will of the AI Athena Parthenus.

Marcia and the Owl paused at the fence that protected the heart of the firebase, this one a simple barrier of wire mesh and lasers, nothing even approaching the height, bulk, and sophistication of the Girding Wall. A lieutenant and two squads of infantry stood at the gate waiting for them.

"I'm to perform a search, ma'am," the lieutenant said.

Marcia waved a hand at the Owl, but the squads split, one sergeant leading her charges toward Marcia herself. The woman at least had the good sense to look worried.

Marcia waved again, and the approaching squad halted. In more or less good order.

"Lieutenant, what are your exact orders?" she asked.

"Um," the man said. "I'm to determine that the prisoner is unarmed and that . . . and that you have not been compromised."

The Owl spread her arms, her cloak flowing from her shoulders to her waist in such a way that it appeared she was about to take flight. "I am not armed," she said. "I need to see whichever Federal rules here."

Marcia stared down the lieutenant.

"I am not compromised," she said. "And I need to go kick the ass of that same Federal."

The lieutenant stood aside.

A few moments later, Marcia led the Owl down the dugout steps to the major's underground command post.

The major was sitting on a camp stool next to a battery-powered lantern that threw up angled shadows on the dirt walls. He was thumbing through one of the moldering fashion magazines a scouting party had uncovered in an abandoned house to the northeast.

He held it up as the two women, soldier and scholar, came to stand before him. The slick paper reflected the light from the lamp, but Marcia could see that the picture he was showing them was of a gazelle-like woman wearing a flowing, high-waisted dress.

"Look how women dressed before Athena's war," he said.

There was no response. Marcia had never dressed like that. She doubted the Owl had either.

The major dropped the magazine onto a stack of others like it and picked up a mug of reconstituted powdered milk. The milk, like the walrus mustache that was immediately dripping white, like the magazines, like the notion that he held any real authority over Marcia, his supposed second, was an affectation. The major's affectations outnumbered his other qualities.

The Owl said, "An Expeditionary Force fighter/bomber has gone down south of the Wall."

The major snorted into the milk he was drinking.

"Every day," he said. "At least one of those flying fools goes down to a bear or some invisible cloud out of

Knoxville every damned day. This is what you risked being shot to come here and tell us?"

He caught Marcia's eye and gave her one of the com-
plicated hand signs he imagined that she had memorized.
She stared back at him steadily until he snorted again.
"The captain here will see you out."

"This fighter/bomber is mostly intact," the Owl said
calmly. She had not removed her helmet with its enormous goggled eyes, despite numerous requests. The
membranes that coated them opened and closed with an
audible clicking sound. "The flying fool is alive, as yet
uncorrupted by Athena, and moving toward the Girding
Wall with the craft's command core."

Marcia hoped she didn't look as agog as the major
at this intelligence, but she was most definitely startled.
"They're supposed to suicide if they go down. And those
cores are designed to self-destruct under any duress.
They're the most sophisticated technology in the federal
arsenal."

The major nodded, agreeing with her for once.

"Neither of those protocols were enacted in this case,"
the Owl replied. "It is our belief that a higher protocol
overrode those and that the pilot is acting on orders he
received even as his plane fell."

"How could you possibly know that?" the major
sputtered.

The Owl answered with the predictable, infuriating response her kin always gave when challenged on their pronouncements. "We know things," she said.

And as events played out, this proved true. The landline to Lexington was up, had been up, in fact, for a remarkable three days running, very nearly a record. So, the major kicked the question of what to do up the chain of command a few steps, then kicked the answer down exactly one step, to Marcia.

So now here she was, with a hand-picked squad of a dozen commandos armed with any and everything the infantry had ever found to be at least temporarily effective against the bizarre forces of the Voluntary State. Here she was with an Owl who claimed to know how to pierce the Girding Wall in a way that let them pass south without anything from beyond passing north. Here she was with orders to rescue an impossibly alive downed pilot carrying the highest technology possessed by the Federals, and further, stricter orders not to question, not to even *wonder* why.

The familiar low hum of the Wall was almost inaudible, riding beneath the cacophony from the foot of the mountain on the other side in a way that Marcia felt with her teeth more than she heard with her ears. She and the troops under her command were as protected as anyone in the Expeditionary Force could be against what they were about to face, should the Owl make good on her promise to see them safely through the barrier. They breathed only the air they carried in tanks on their backs. They saw only what the micro-cameras atop their helmets relayed in to their blacked-out goggles.

They sang no songs.

Now close enough to the Wall to touch it, the Owl stopped, lying sprawled out on her belly with her mottled cape spread over her back. Marcia clicked her tongue twice and when the commandos arrayed in a prone semi-circle behind her immediately stopped crawling forward, she knew that their communications net, at least, was still uncorrupted.

"Captain," said the Owl, her voice as calm and level as ever. "Your blade, please."

The question briefly confused Marcia. Did this woman think they were going into the Voluntary State armed with *swords*?

Then she saw the Owl put her hands together and mime opening something. So Marcia ripped open the hook and eye clasps of her fatigues' thigh pouch and handed over her folding knife.

The woman, the *witch* woman Marcia thought before pushing the ridiculous thought down, opened the knife. The blade was a scant three inches long. Did she think she was going to use it to cut through a structure woven of numbers and steel ten yards thick?

But the Owl did not extend the hand that held Marcia's knife toward the Girding Wall. Instead, she dipped her head, reached up, and neatly snipped a brown and white feather from her helmet. She then folded the knife closed almost primly, almost delicately, and offered it back to Marcia.

Taking the knife and resecuring her thigh pouch, Marcia signaled her soldiers to stand since the Owl was doing so. She saw them running their hands over their weapons and equipment, making tactile checks of what their eyes could only see secondhand.

The Owl raised her hand as high as she could. She pressed the tip of the feather against the surface of the Wall and spoke in a screeching voice, words that were both familiar and incomprehensible to Marcia.

"Let in equal the square root of negative infinity let in let in let in . . ."

A white light shone where the feather touched, no, where it *pierced* the Wall. The light persisted in a liquid trail as the Owl swept her arm around, inscribing a circle. The bluish-black surface of the Wall within the circle shimmered and danced like a pool of mercury held impossibly upright.

"Now, Captain," said the Owl, and stepped through.

Marcia subvocalized, "Go, go, go."

And they went.

And they went into madness.

Years later, when she was to be discharged after the war had come to an end no one found satisfactory, Marcia was interviewed by a number of blue-uniformed men wearing insignia she did not recognize. They called her in to question her account of the failed rescue and recovery mission and those of the other two soldiers who had survived the encounter with the gaunt, eight-foot-tall thing that the downed pilot had become after being possessed by Athena's will.

They pointed out the inconsistencies among the testimonies of the three of them, and somehow made Marcia feel guilty that she had neither hung herself nor walked naked and weeping into the Green River, as the other two had done in the months after they had followed the Owl of the Bluegrass, in the soldier savant's dying act, back through the Girding Wall.

"You mentioned floating green spheres. 'Green spheres everywhere,' you said in your account. But neither Sergeant Filson nor Corporal Tell reported anything about them."

Marcia shrugged. "They both swallowed them. Maybe that made them forget."

"Corporal Tell wrote in his diary that you . . . wait, I'll just read it. 'The captain killed it with our breath. Then she breathed it.' What does that mean?"

Marcia stared at the ceiling for a long, long minute.

Then she asked, "Are you going to discharge me?"

They did.

NOW

Marcia's more or less amiable relationship with her ex-husband meant she didn't bother knocking at his door in the courthouse annex. When she went in, the office was empty except for the three or four cats he kept around the place.

As sheriff and jailer both, he was probably serving lunch to whomever he had in lockup that day. Marcia didn't mind waiting. She went over to the bookshelves to see if Carter had made any new acquisitions since she'd last visited him.

No new books, but, as always, there was the elaborate, black-feathered headdress taking pride of place amid the volumes of history and anthropology. It was fashioned to look like a crow's head.

She lifted it off the shelf and studied it with some distaste. She felt an unaccountable urge to put the thing on, but then contented herself with simply examining its interior.

"Brings back old times, doesn't it?"

Carter was standing at the door, his enormous halo of kinky white hair a stark contrast to his dark skin. He wore an apron over his uniform. It hadn't protected his sheriff's star from getting speckled with gravy.

"How did you *see* out of this thing?" she asked, putting the helmet back in its place.

"Most of the time I was wearing one I was running like hell from some kind of nanotech nightmare," said Carter. "I only needed to see straight ahead."

"Dressing up like birds to fight an impossible army," said Marcia. "You people were lunatics."

Carter took off the apron and hung it on one of a row of hooks screwed into the wall. The next one along held a holster, which in turn held a pistol Marcia knew for a fact had never been fired in the line of duty. It hadn't even been loaded in years.

"Wasn't you federal troops that ended the war, though, was it? Speaking of your former colleagues, I've got a note here that says I'm one of them, now. County militia's been federalized, along with everything else. Does that make me your superior officer?"

Marcia gave him a look that she'd practiced all through both of their marriages.

"Nah, I'm just kidding," said Carter. "The only things I'm your superior at are cooking and telling jokes."

He wasn't actually all that good at either of those, but he was telling the truth.

"Did your message tell you what they're up to?" she asked him.

Carter shook his head and walked to his round desk, which consisted of a gigantic spool salvaged from an old strip mine site. "All I know is that I'm supposed to ensure unit discipline and readiness, which is kind of hilarious, and that our next paychecks will be issued in federal dollars, which will be nice come Christmas. I might get the girls some things."

The girls were the cats.

"There's already another unit of troops in the county, Carter. They've been here for two weeks. Or at least they were dropped in two weeks ago. Nobody's heard from them since they sent one message saying they'd landed safely."

"Landed safely where?" he asked.

Marcia said, "Back near the Gap. Back home."

Carter started humming to himself as he picked up a folder thick with printouts, set it down, picked it up again. Here, all at once, were three habits that had charmed her before their first marriage, irritated her during their second, and now, all these years later, were things to simply accept if she was to accept him as part of her life in any capacity.

Humming as he gathered his thoughts, ramping up to some decisive pronouncement that brooked no argument. Expending resources on ephemera like physical media because he was so tactile, his short, thick fingers so surprisingly sensitive to temperature, to timbre, to touch. Picking things up and putting them down. "He's always *fiddling* with things," Marcia's mother would have said, had she ever met Carter.

The humming stopped.

She looked over to see his unlined face bearing the expression she knew it would. Resolve.

"No," he said.

Marcia shrugged. "There's no one else."

"There's *me*. I'm the sheriff. I'm the one with the federal commission, as of an hour ago, anyway. I'm the one with a gun."

Marcia fought back a smirk, which was difficult, but she knew if she let one quirk her lips what was about to follow would take even longer. That the inevitable argument, which as far as she was concerned, he had been the one to start in this instance, would take even more time.

"What do you think there is to shoot up there?" she asked him. She kept her voice low and even, which wasn't as bad as a smirk, but was close.

Carter ignored her tone. He was ramping up all right. "I counted thirteen special forces types out there, led by a captain where there should be a lieutenant. All armed for war. What do *they* think there is to shoot up there?"

She considered not telling him. But the possibility existed that he already knew, that he'd been planning on offering his services as a guide to the Federals and not telling her about it. Much more likely, though, he had simply intuited what the captain believed was hidden in the uplands.

After all, he knew Athena Parthenus and her works at least as well as she did.

The silence she met his question with extended. They had both long since grown comfortable with uncomfortable silences.

This time, it was him who broke it.

"I can activate your commission," he said. "I can give you an order."

Marcia just looked at him. She wondered if he really had it in him to do that. She was saddened that he had it in him to even suggest it.

Carter must have thought through what he had just said, though. Regret flashed in his eyes and he changed tack. "I can deputize you. Put you in charge of the county's security while I'm up there."

Marcia was suddenly overcome with a powerful feeling of . . . what? Regret? Nostalgia? She thought of an old, potent question. What kind of father would this man have made? If she hadn't been sterilized when she was drafted, if the thousand war orphans in this county where they'd settled hadn't been spirited away east, if, if, if.

What difference did it make? Why was she thinking of this now?

Another titanic argument needed attending to, latest in an endless series. But before she unleashed on him, she said, "Carter. You can let me go."

He had been about to sit down. Instead, he picked a cat up from the top of a cabinet and walked over to stand before the crow helmet. The cat eyed the odd artifact, a growl growing down in its throat. Her master, her *friend* he always said of his relationship with them, was holding his head at a slight angle, as if listening to the cat with all the intent he could muster.

Finally, he spoke. "You should take my gun."

She felt no impulse to smirk. She smiled, sadly. "Do you have any ammunition?" she asked.

He was still staring at the old helmet, stroking the cat into calmness.

"No," he said. "Not for a long time, now."

The history of the Crow Band (or Bands) is complex. While it has been suggested that the first Crows were active before the rise of Athena Parthenus, the dating of those early accounts is complicated and frequently contradictory. What is known with more certainty is that they were only reluctant allies to the federal forces that eventually took full governance of the Commonwealth of Kentucky, and while there are no known instances of outright armed clashes between the military and paramilitary organizations, the Crows had no qualms about raiding federal warehouses and even firebases for supplies.

—*A History of the First Athena War*

A LONG TIME AGO

Marcia and her undermanned platoon were on patrol along the banks of the Cumberland River, equipped with guns that shot fire instead of bullets or the more exotic ammunition they were sometimes issued, and which was sometimes efficacious against invasive threats.

For all the work and treasure that had gone into the building of the Girding Wall, for all the genius of structural and software engineering that had accomplished the black and blue vastness of the barely understandable thing, the Federals who built it had not managed to reroute the river.

So it flowed south under the Wall and, according to maps Marcia had seen and dim memories of lessons from her school days before the war, before Athena Parthenus's ascension in Nashville, it flowed back north again under the Wall away west, transformed into something potent and strange by its flow through the Voluntary State.

Marcia had heard rumors that the Cumberland was

not the only waterway in the Commonwealth polluted by Athena's inhuman wiles and subverting wares, but here on the plateau, at least, the river was safe. That safety depended on filters under the water, which were designed like one-way valves to keep out invasive species, and in the main they worked, at least against what passed for fauna from south of the Wall.

Flora were a different story.

Their orders were to scout both sides of the river in an overlapping grid pattern from the Wall upstream three klicks, where the Corps of Engineers maintained a pontoon bridge over the wild river. The Cumberland had been a slack thing in this country once, streaming between two impounded lakes. The dams, though, had been destroyed by bombarding bears—those semi-sentient balloon creatures from the skies above Tennessee—long since.

Specifically, the troops were to "locate, identify, map, and destroy any incursive plant life or similar." The plant life was why the platoon was equipped with four flamethrowers. The "similar" was why they all wore goggles and micropore masks.

The soldiers under her command called the duty "weed eating."

One of the sergeants came to her now. His voice was muffled by his mask, so he spoke loudly and forcefully. It occurred to Marcia that the man always spoke loudly and forcefully. A sergeant to his boots.

"Company, Lieutenant. Partisan."

"Partisans" were what the intelligence people safely bunkered at the Expeditionary Force's headquarters near Lexington called the Crow Bands and their allies. Most of the troops just called them the locals, because with the depopulation of the border regions exemplified by the abandoned town of Albany where the platoon was bivouacked, the only Kentuckians they ever encountered were the strange guerrilla fighters.

Marcia kept her own background as a native daughter quiet, though of course it was noted in her service jacket and so discoverable by any of her superiors. None of them had ever mentioned it.

The platoon had come to a halt on the degrading road they were marching along. The west side of the lane fell off in a tumble of rocks and fallen timber. The east side, to their right, rose sharply and was heavily forested. Both sides were choked with kudzu, but kudzu was not the kind of invasive species they were detailed to deal with.

Before them, a lithe woman stood alone in the middle of the road. She wore the Crow Band's regalia, a feathered helmet shaped to tightly enclose a human head and conceal human features, but with meticulously designed elements that evoked corvids, along with a feathered cape of glossy black that was rumored to offer some protection against the coherent light beams some creatures of the Voluntary State could spit like venom.

The plastic armor Marcia and her troops wore offered no such protection.

The woman was leaning on an old hunting rifle, the open end of the barrel acting as the foot of a crutch, its stock stuck under her arm. Marcia wondered what would happen if the woman tried to fire such a laxly kept weapon, but elected to follow protocol for such an encounter.

"We're the second platoon of Charlie Company, stationed at Firebase Corbin. We were told you people were concentrating your . . . efforts farther west."

The woman reached up and made quick work of the complicated clasps and buckles at her chin and ears. She unceremoniously let her rifle fall to the ground and lifted off her helmet with both hands. She had mousy brown hair, a sharp nose, and was shockingly pale skinned, as if she were an underground dweller like the civilians said to be sheltering in the caves north of Bowling Green, or as if she were some kind of nocturnal creature. Or as if she seldom took off her helmet.

"We weren't doing any good," she said, her accent so familiar to Marcia. "Do y'all think you're doing any good?" She laughed then, a surprisingly delightful sound.

"Don't mock them, Alma." This was a man's voice, and even though his words clearly constituted an order, there was laughter in them, too.

Suddenly, there was movement all along the upward slope, a dozen masked and cloaked figures rising out of the weeds. Marcia heard her platoon behind her moving, knew they were hitting the deck, raising rifles, establishing fields of fire.

"Hold up," she said, turning her head to one side against the muffling of her own mask, and raising one hand. "Hold up."

It was clear which of the suddenly revealed figures had spoken. He was broad-shouldered and shorter than Marcia, who was not an unusually tall woman. His rifle, she noted, was slung over one shoulder and appeared to her practiced eye to be in good working order.

The man stepped out onto the road. Given the stumbling Marcia and her troops made of their cross-country efforts, she wondered at his grace.

He lifted off his helmet. He was a Black man with a shaved skull, and he had the greenest eyes Marcia had ever seen.

"Alma's being rude, and I apologize for that, Lieutenant. But truth be told, we've been watching you for two days now, and you've left a lot of Athena's filth growing behind you."

Then he smiled broadly and offered Marcia his hand. "My name is Carter," he said.

NOW

"I'm glad I didn't have to draft you," said the captain. He signed something and moved it to one side. The fuselage of the ugly warship was barracks, mess hall, and platoon headquarters all in one. Marcia didn't recognize half of the machines purring along the interior walls. Some of them looked suspiciously . . . organic to her.

"There's nobody else," she said. Nobody else she'd let go.

"We'll leave as soon as we can get a detail of dependents trained to carry the excess gear," said the captain. "Do you think you can help with that? The sergeant's been drilling a whole gang of them all morning, but she says she isn't getting anywhere."

"Drilling?" asked Marcia. "You people are trying to instill military discipline in little harvesters?" She choked back a laugh.

"I'm under orders to make full use of local assets and personnel, Agent," said the captain. "I'm not sure which of those categories these dependents you Westerners suffer to live among fall under, but they're certainly one of them."

Marcia's good humor evaporated. "We Westerners suffer to live among the dependents because you Easterners sent them to us," she said coldly. "It's what you did to meet the repopulation quotas instead of moving west of the mountains yourselves."

The captain matched her stare evenly. Then he said, "You were once briefly a brevet major, so I'll be courteous. I was born in Jacksonville, and I was living there when Athena sent the Commodores Lambent and Brother Fortran to level the city. My entire family was killed, and I was injured to such a point that about sixty percent of my body is made up of the same monotissue that your harvesters and teamsters and so on are grown from."

It was a war story. A war story about the hulking Commodores, the creators of and creations of Athena who were so terrible and powerful that the Queen of Reason had only dared bring thirty-six of them into existence.

Marcia had heard plenty of war stories about Commodores. She had one herself. "What's your point?" she asked.

"My point is that I was a child and so I couldn't come then," said the captain. "My point is that I've come now."

As the AI did with other institutions of the original "Volunteer State," Athena converted a remnant of the Tennessee State Police into an internal security force deployed to quell dissent (this usually involved sedition or outright rebellion among the rock monkeys across the Mississippi River in Arkansas). The TSP did, however, have a role in offensive operations against the Federals and their allies, the infamous Bears in the Air.

—*A History of the First Athena War*

A LONG TIME AGO

Because she could see nothing, hear nothing, feel nothing but cool water lapping at her in the tank, Marcia survived.

The orders for the soldiery posted to Firebase Corbin indicated that the major should be the first to enter the subterranean tank, newly installed in a pit dug by hand. The embodied communications devices they'd heard so many rumors about had finally reached their part of the front, and being ensconced in the sense-depriving environment of the tank was the final step in their integration.

The major thought it best if Marcia go first. She had read the orders—she always read the orders from Lexington even when the major did not—but shrugged off his subversion of them. The way she always did.

So she had stripped to her olive-green underwear, swallowed the two-centimeter capsule that looked and tasted like stainless steel and felt like it going down, and turned her head from side to side so that the doctor who'd come to administer the treatments could spray a cold mist into her ear canals.

Then she went into the tank and was there for what seemed like a very long time. Eventually, the blossoming feelings in her gut and in her head subsided, and the automatic functions of the tank popped its clasps. She climbed out to find no one waiting for her.

She ascended the stairs of the deep dugout to find ravenous bears floating above the shattered remains of the firebase.

Marcia ducked back, flattening herself against the steps. Bears hadn't come over the Girding Wall this far east for years, not since they had spent months dropping defoliants and other poisons on the mountains to ease the passage of Athena's coal moles. Not since the Federals had sortied thousands of fighters against the bears and thousands of bombers against the moles.

She had never heard of them coming this close to the ground.

A shadow traveled slowly across the upper stairs, as something vast and slow occluded the setting sun. The angle of the light told Marcia that she had been in the tank for at least twelve hours. How long after she'd gone in had the bears descended?

How had they not found her? Bears were said to have

preternatural senses, able to sniff out targets from above the clouds with their bulbous noses.

She felt an enormous pressure behind her eyes then. Marcia had never had a migraine, but the dark spots that appeared at the center of her field of vision might be explained by one.

That wasn't it, of course. She put a hand to her forehead as the shadow moved on. The pressure behind her eyes moved on, as well.

Marcia had been this close to one of the more potent of Athena's minions only once before, and that had been an occasion of tragedy. Now she lay on mud stairs topped with particle board, dripping wet and nearly naked. Unarmed and ignorant of what was going on above.

A message from nowhere flashed into her consciousness. *Artillery inbound. Take cover.*

Even as she struggled to make sense of the disembodied voice, she heard the telltale whistling of the shells. The Expeditionary Force had taken control of and retasked the big guns used by the Postal Service long since.

After, when she crawled out of the dugout, she only found evidence that one bear had been hit, its deflated skin already melting into the ground. She searched the darkening sky but saw nothing but the emerging stars.

Most of the deployment was under the tarp that had roofed the mess hall. The major's ridiculous mustache was caked with blood. His eyes, all their eyes, had boiled away.

Another message.

Frocked acting major. No attendant change in pay grade or allowances. Take command of Firebase Corbin and await further orders.

There was nobody to detail to burial duty but herself. Marcia went in search of an entrenching tool.

NOW

The platoon's sergeant was a rectangular Black woman called Moss, and for all that the soldiers watched her tiniest expression for guidance, the captain had been right about her getting nowhere with the dependents.

Eleven bright green little harvesters and one silo hand—Marcia was almost positive they were the same ones who had warned her about the ship the previous afternoon—were crawling all over a disordered heap of boxes, backpacks, and bags. They were whispering their nonsense words and tossing the contents of the packages back and forth. One of them had figured out how to open a ration pack and a small group was examining the contents studiously, sniffing and giggling, but not touching the gray stuff.

Sergeant Moss had detailed a couple of corporals to work with the dependents, to instill order, Marcia supposed. One of these, a tall, thin, painfully young man, was pacing back and forth with a bewildered look on his face. The other, a rotund woman with short-cropped hair, had apparently given up on the dependents and was simply moving from pile to pile, repacking things.

The sergeant appeared next to Marcia. "Do they even understand English?" she asked.

Marcia eyed the other woman. Sergeant Moss was *solid*, her impressive physique lending her much in the way of gravitas, but her tone was frustrated.

"Sure they do," Marcia answered. "What did you ask them to do?"

"They've been drafted," said Moss. "I *told* them to ready that gear for porting."

Marcia studied the chaotic scene again. "Well," she said. "That's what they're doing."

"They're making a mess of everything!" protested Moss. "They keep unpacking the containers and making little piles."

"And you should let them keep doing that. Have you *counted* the piles?"

The sergeant looked flummoxed, but then studied the area. "Twelve," she said.

"Right," said Marcia. "You want them to haul all this stuff for you, but obviously those backpacks won't fit them. They're individually stronger than me—probably stronger than you—but the gear isn't packaged in a way that's efficient for them to carry. So they're repackaging it."

The sergeant's expression had gone from bewildered frustration to cautious curiosity.

"Are you sure?" she asked.

"They were designed for efficient manual labor," said Marcia.

"Why didn't they just tell me what they were doing?"

One of the little harvesters examining the ration pack stepped forward and resealed it, then tossed it onto one of the dozen piles. All the others except the silo hand whistled in unison.

"They *did* tell you," Marcia said.

A LONG TIME AGO

Marcia stood with her husband and her eldest cousin, the three of them comprising most of the county's government as well as, she supposed, an ad hoc welcoming committee for the hundreds of . . . beings that now crowded the landing field at the edge of town. Two federal mass conveyors, bellies open, crouched along the north side of the field, and their squat, bizarrely colored passengers spread out from them like clouds of dye poured in clear water.

"You checked again?" asked Carter.

Annoyed, Marcia nevertheless nodded. "Nothing more from Frankfort, nothing more from the Federals. Just the same four-page document they sent after the Reseeding. These ... *dependents* are to act as laborers ahead of an eventual resettlement from the East."

"We need more people," said Marcia's cousin, Roger, an elderly white man with more hair in his ears than on his head. He had been elected county judge when Marcia had made it clear that she would not serve in that capacity.

Sometimes she regretted that decision. Serving as the Commonwealth's county agent saw her working six days out of seven most weeks, whereas Roger had made the judgeship a strictly part-time position. He spent most of his time tending to the spiritual needs of a slowly dwindling flock of Free Will Baptists, whom he preached to once on Wednesdays and twice on Sundays.

One of the less fractious arguments Marcia and Carter regularly indulged in was a game of semantics. Was Roger's executive authority in the county an example of hierocracy or of gerontocracy?

Staring at the mass of new-come creatures, she realized that she couldn't remember which position she had taken the last time they'd fought over it. It didn't really matter.

"Well," said Carter, "I guess here are more people, then."

Roger turned the sheriff a myopic eye. "These aren't people, son. They're stamped-out machines, little different than the creatures of the demon queen."

The demon queen was the sobriquet Roger used for Athena Parthenus. During the war, he'd preached that she was the Anti-Christ come to signal the end of days, but after her destruction, he'd changed his mind for reasons having to do with theology and prophecy that he and Carter sometimes debated during their checkers games. Carter was not a believer, but he was a reader. Marcia avoided those conversations.

"You know they're not machines, Judge," said Carter. That he'd called the old man Judge meant he was in a foul mood.

Well, so was Marcia.

"Where are we supposed to put them?" she wondered aloud. "What are we supposed to feed them? Do they even eat?"

Suddenly, answers came, so swiftly and of such a comprehensive nature that she staggered. Her embodied comms unit, dormant now for years, was flooded with data.

"What is it?" asked Carter, clearly aware that his wife

was enduring something strange and unwelcome. "What's wrong?"

Marcia took a deep breath and realized that the two men were supporting her, each holding her up by one arm. "Preprogrammed data dump," she said, falling back on terminology from her time in the military. "Tight beamed from one of those ships. God, there's a manifest. They're listed like cargo."

There was little doubt on either man's face who—or what—she meant by "they're."

"Machines," said Roger again.

Carter, thankfully, ignored that.

"What else have you learned?" he asked. "How are we supposed to take care of them?"

Marcia shook her head. "We're not," she said. "They're going to take care of themselves. Look." She pointed across the field.

Many of the bright green dependents—Marcia knew now that their specialization was as harvesters of the grain crops that had grown since the Reseeding and which had thus far gone untended for lack of hands for the tending—along with some fewer with skin tones of violet, had suddenly coalesced from a milling mob into plumb-line straight rows running from the cargo lifts of the conveyors to an empty marshaling yard along one side of the field.

Even as the three of them watched, bundles and crates far larger than Marcia would have guessed the little creatures could maneuver unaided were handed swiftly down each line. Other dependents of various hues organized and opened the crates with alarming speed and efficiency.

Poles went up, followed by the plastic tarp roofing of the type used in the refugee shelters in the first days of the war. Some sort of vehicle was being assembled under the largest tent.

All of this was done in absolute silence.

"Are they children?" Roger asked after it eventually became apparent that the work they were watching was going to go on for a long time. Apparent, too, that his cousin wasn't going to volunteer any specifics on her own.

"They're all exactly eighteen months old," Marcia answered him.

"Then yes," said Roger.

"No," said Marcia. "They're fully mature."

"I can't even tell the men from the women."

Marcia shook her head. "They're not gendered. And there won't be any children. They're incapable of reproduction."

Roger made a disgusted sound, then spoke, his voice taking on a different timbre. "So God created man in his own image, in the image of God created he him; male and female created he them."

The vehicle, Marcia now saw, was a bus. She remembered a ride to a camp, the person who shared her seat the first person she'd ever met who was neither male nor female.

"I don't know, old man," said Carter.

"Don't know what?"

Marcia was embarrassed that she and Roger had answered simultaneously and identically.

"Colossians instead of Genesis," Carter answered them both. "All things were created by him, and for him."

NOW

The platoon, under the direction of Sergeant Moss, and the little harvesters, under the apparent direction of the silo hand, were ready to go about two hours before sunset.

"We can get to the edge of the quarantine zone, anyway," the captain said, looking at one of his finely detailed maps. "Then we head into the uplands at dawn."

Marcia thought the plan foolish, but representative of the whole project, and she'd already made her decision about the larger enterprise, so she kept silent. She hoisted the pack she carried on fishing trips, lighter than the kits carried by the soldiers, lighter by *far* than what the little harvesters bore, and headed down the gravel road that ran southeast out of town. After a moment, she heard Sergeant Moss call for the party to march.

Marcia set a moderate pace. She knew for a fact that the little harvesters had the endurance to march for days, and the soldiers were certainly in better shape than she. She had to be careful of her knees. And wasn't in any particular hurry.

Either the captain had guessed she'd go easy, or he'd been conservative in his estimate of how long it would take them to reach the quarantine zone, because there was still a quarter hour's light left when the gravel road abruptly stopped at the edge of a gully. Marcia hoped that both things were true, as that would indicate a canniness in the man that might help keep them alive in the uplands.

The champagne cork pop sound of tents being hatched and the low hum of chemical stoves competed with scarce mountain night noises. The permanent cloud cover hung low. The captain found Marcia in front of her tent and invited himself to sit down. At least this time he didn't take the best spot.

"I visited your friend the sheriff this afternoon," he said. "Interesting man. Not many people of his former affiliation serving in law enforcement, I don't think."

Marcia almost said that she and Carter weren't exactly friends, but then she decided that wasn't exactly true, so she decided not to say anything at all. This didn't discourage the captain from speaking on.

"He showed me an old map of this area," he said. "Can you believe these old hills used to be covered with trees?"

Marcia could *remember* when at least some of the hills had been covered with trees.

"That's what they came for first," she said.

"That's what *who* came for first?" asked the captain.

"Outsiders. You. Us. Did you know that the whole edge of the escarpment through here was a sort of second Fertile Crescent? A new world one. A forest one."

"What do you mean?"

"Some of those old books of Carter's tell the story. Before the maize revolution, before the three sisters came up from the south, there was something like agriculture here. Plant management of some kind, anyway, based on seeds and nuts and tubers. Grasses. Maybe fungus, too, but evidence of that couldn't survive to be recorded."

"The ground's still fertile," said the captain. "Thus, the Reseeding."

"The ground's *fertilized*," said Marcia. "What's left of it. These mountains—this run of these mountains—weren't permanently occupied when the Europeans first came in

61

numbers, hadn't been for a long time. Settlement patterns were such that poor Scots Irish and African slaves came first and made what we later thought of as Appalachian culture, which for a long time was based on subsistence agriculture and limited timbering. Then they came and started taking the trees."

"Them again," said the captain mildly.

"Yes, them. Extractors."

The captain gave her a sharp look at the word.

"The trees, then the minerals, then the mountains themselves in search of more minerals. These hills are a place people come to take things away."

"And I suppose there's a lesson in that about what we're doing?"

Marcia shook her head. "Nobody else has ever learned any lessons from it. I don't know why we should be any different."

A LONG TIME AGO

In the days before they began what Marcia imagined must surely have been one of the largest-scale landscaping efforts ever undertaken by humanity, before they began the project that rivaled the remaking of Tennessee into the Voluntary

State by decidedly inhuman hands, the Federals sent flights of drones low over all the counties fronting the escarpment. They dropped slips of plasticized paper wherever people or manmade structures were detected. The papers drifted down like the snow said to once blanket the hills in wintertime, and this is what they said:

> *Attention! / ¡Atención!*
> *Heed! / ¡Atención!*
> *Mark Well These Words! / ¡Recuerden bien*
> *   estas palabras!*
> *Seek Shelter Tonight! / ¡Busquen refugio esta*
> *   noche!*
> *Stay Sheltered Until The Clouds Subside! /*
> *   ¡Quédense en refugio hasta que las nubes*
> *   desaparezcan!*

There was a drought on. There hadn't been a cloud in the sky for weeks.

Then, the morning after the leaflets had been dropped and their warning had either been assiduously followed, as in the case of most of the county's six hundred residents, or studiously ignored, as in the case of Marcia and, she noted with some distaste, her estranged husband, who was keeping to the opposite side of the dry courthouse yard, clouds *did* come.

First, clouds of ships.

No low and fast-moving drones, these, but sun-blotting mass lifters in numbers Marcia had not thought existed anymore. They floated above, silent in their altitude, then cracked open their fuselages and let loose the second wave of clouds.

Came the rain, but . . .

"Get inside!" Marcia shouted to Carter as the first sizzling yellow drops struck the parched earth.

It had lately been his habit to ignore her when she raised her voice. But he nodded, and then disappeared into the courthouse annex. Marcia, farther from shelter, ran toward the portico of the main building, her boots splashing in the puddles that were already forming.

The smell that accompanied the rain was acrid and chemical. But that was secondary to what Marcia saw in the hills beyond what remained of the town. The rainfall there was such a torrent that it seemed a solid rush of water, or whatever the yellow stuff was. Through the intervening distance, Marcia watched the hillsides washed clean away into the gullies and valleys, right down to the blistered bedrock.

She retreated into the courthouse and sought the upper floors.

After water, earth.

The day after the rains, the choking clouds that came

were of fine black soil dropped from the same ships that flooded the county. Again, the heaviest loads were dropped in the hills where the fertilized, seeded, programmed matrix made a new topography.

The haze did not subside for days.

After it did, Carter and Marcia made a circuit of the county, counting the dead. It would only be later they realized that their marriage died during those traumatic rounds.

By the time of the last burials, burials dug into ground turned alien and strange, the green shoots of wheat-like plant life were thick on the hillsides, nearly knee high.

The second snow of fliers came just as the first kernels of grain were budding. Few of the survivors bothered to read about the best practices for harvesting the perennial subversion of evolution.

This was the Reseeding.

NOW

Marcia woke to the sound of voices raised in anger. She started to roll to her feet, then stopped, cursing what the damp night air had done to her muscles, and stretched. As least the air mattress built into the floor of her tent meant she hadn't slept on the ground, so her back wasn't too bad.

She pulled on her boots and clambered out of the tent. The sun hadn't peeked over the tops of the hills, but the sky was lightening, pale blue streaked with white. It was still cool.

The shouting was coming from the far edge of the camp, where the little harvesters had pitched the lean-to they'd all slept in. The voice belonged to Sergeant Moss.

"I'm going to ask you one more time! Where are they?"

Marcia found nearly the whole platoon gathered in a semicircle around the sergeant. The captain, drinking from a steaming insulated mug, stood off to one side. The silo hand stood blinking up at Sergeant Moss.

"What's happened?" Marcia asked. She pitched her voice loud enough for the whole group to hear.

The captain looked over, almost casually, and said nothing. Sergeant Moss snapped her head around and was about to speak when the silo hand broke into a run. They avoided the soldiers grabbing for them and skidded to a stop behind Marcia. She looked down at them and they pointed at the sergeant.

Moss was approaching, the pure physical threat of the woman unlike anything Marcia had experienced in years.

"Hold, Sergeant," said the captain. "The agent asked a

question. Answer her."

Moss visibly forced herself to relax. "Those little bastards ran off in the night and took half our gear with them is what happened."

Marcia looked at the silo hand again. They looked up at her gravely, then, surprising her, nodded once.

"You didn't have sentries set?" asked Marcia.

"Of course we did," said the sergeant. "They apparently slept through the whole thing. They're *still* asleep, can't be roused. They must have been drugged."

Marcia doubted that. "Your pharmech doesn't detect anything, though, does it?" The sergeant wouldn't have said "must have been" if she knew for sure.

The soldier who served as the unit's medic held up the sleek device from where it was slung around his shoulder. "Just said they were in REM sleep." He checked a reading. "They still are. Have been ever since I checked them almost an hour ago."

"And who knows how long before that?" asked the captain. "Sergeant, have you surveyed what they took?"

"Hardware," said the sergeant. "Tech stuff. They left all the food and water. Didn't touch the spare weapons or ammo, either. Just things like the backup pharmech and the radio set."

Marcia was surprised by that last item. She assumed that all the soldiers, like herself, had surgically implanted comms gear. Radio had proven worse than useless during the war, detectable as it was by any receiver. Coded transmissions were instantly cracked by Athena's minions, so the army had adapted the enemy's own technology and developed the forebrain communications devices. Marcia only dimly understood how they worked. She'd heard that the surgeons and scientists didn't understand them much better.

The captain guessed what she was thinking. "The radio is a backup. Since the extraction team went offline, one theory is that our embodied communications have been compromised."

Marcia shrugged that off. "Where did they go?"

Moss said, "How should we know? That's what I'm trying to get out of your friend, there."

"Eleven dependents carrying packs and traveling by night," said Marcia. "Yes, how could you possibly know?"

She walked over to the backside of the lean-to, the silo hand shadowing her closely. She cast her eyes over the ground. The signs were obvious to her.

"They went ahead," she said. "They headed into the hills."

The captain nodded and started to say something, but he was interrupted by the shouting medic.

"They're waking up!"

As it turned out, though, the pair of soldiers who'd

slept through their shifts remembered nothing but vivid, and oddly similar, dreams.

"I kept opening my head to try to call somebody," one of them said. "That doesn't make any sense, does it? Opening my head?"

There was no discussion about returning to town. As soon as the camp was packed up, the captain gave the order to march. Sergeant Moss stayed conspicuously close to the silo hand, who in turn never drifted more than a few feet from Marcia.

They spent the morning walking up a dry creek bed. Marcia could see that the little harvesters has passed the same way just a few hours before.

The captain made his way up from the center of the column to walk beside her.

"All these old creek beds make for easy walking," he said. "One good thing about there being so little running water in this country."

There used to be creeks and rivers and rills everywhere in the hills.

"They had names," said Marcia.

The captain raised an eyebrow.

"They were called Troublesome and Stinking and Rockcastle. Owl and Muddy and Sulphur and Little Turtle."

The captain said, "And then Athena's burrowers

rerouted the aquifers somehow. There's nothing anybody can do about that."

"We can remember," said Marcia, and quickened her pace.

———————

But the difficulty she was having in guiding the platoon was that she *couldn't* remember. It had been more than forty years since she had last walked these hills, and they had changed even more drastically than she had.

The uplands had once been places of water and wood. Now the hills were treeless tors like something out of an old novel from across the ocean. Low, tough grasses carpeted the hillsides except where the bedrock broke through. There were no birds, no insects, no animals of any kind. Windblown grass and scudding clouds were all the movement they saw besides themselves.

In midafternoon, the captain called a halt and consulted his maps. "We're about four miles from the drop zone the extraction team was assigned. Their target was a farther four miles east. We're not going to make it that far today."

Marcia looked over his shoulder. The map rippled slightly. It was a palimpsest, showing the same territory at different points in time depending on how it was held and manipulated. She saw the Gap clearly. It held steady.

"I can get there today," she said.

The captain and the sergeant exchanged a look Marcia found unreadable.

"I can go ahead and see what's up there," she continued. "Then walk back overnight and report on what I've found."

The captain said, "You weren't a ranger. You were front line infantry."

"I know how to be quiet, and I know how to take observations," said Marcia.

"But you don't know the way," he replied. "You said yourself the landscape has changed too much."

Marcia tapped the map. "I'll take this. Between it and what I *do* remember, I'll find the way."

The captain thought a moment, then said, "Okay. But you're taking Moss with you."

The platoon marched on another half mile, until they found a spot to camp that was, to the sergeant's eye, "defensible." This time, the soldiers didn't immediately set up tents and start cook fires. Instead, they began digging in with entrenching tools. Marcia was almost overcome with a feeling of tainted nostalgia. This is what the war had been like. Men and women carrying incredibly advanced weapons and technology, men and women with incredibly advanced technology grafted within their very bodies and brains, here hacking at the ground with tools that wouldn't have been unfamiliar to soldiers making camp 3,000 years ago.

"Are you ready, Agent?" Sergeant Moss asked. She was bent under an enormous pack and bearing an enormous rifle of a type Marcia hadn't seen before, though she recognized some of the design elements. It was like knowing who a child's grandparents were by the child's eyes and ears.

Marcia slipped her own pack off her shoulders and let it slide to the ground. The closest thing to a weapon she carried was an old folding pocketknife Carter had given her long before their first marriage. It had once belonged to some Crow Band warleader character Carter had been very fond of, and he had made much of the gift. It wasn't a particularly good knife, but it held an edge and she'd never managed to lose it. Maybe it *was* a good knife.

"You're not taking any gear?" asked Moss.

Marcia slapped the sergeant's outsized pack. "Surely there's enough in there for both of us." She went to see that the soldiers watching the silo hand, who the captain had forbidden from accompanying them, weren't being too unkind.

The two women hiked for a couple of hours, stopping once in the extraction team's targeted landing area for a good look around. Neither of them found any signs of

federal soldiers, runaway dependents, or Athenian arti-
facts. Which might mean anything.

"The extraction team would have covered their tracks,"
said Moss, somewhat uneasily.

"If this is even where they landed," said Marcia. The
naked hills had an eerie sameness to them. Marcia
checked the map again. It was stuck on the image of how
the hills had been before the war. She shook it, but it
didn't change.

"We were going that way," she said after a moment.

"How can you even tell?" grumbled the sergeant.

"Because that way is *up*," said Marcia.

An hour later, they came across the first little harvester.
They were curled up in the middle of the streambed, fast
asleep.

Marcia shook their shoulder gently, stopped the
sergeant from trying anything more aggressive. "This is
like your sentries last night, don't you see?"

"We need to wake it up so we can find out where our
gear is."

Something about the little harvester bothered Marcia,
though. Something wasn't quite right about their clothes
or complexion.

"Sergeant, do you have a reader in that pack?"

"Of course." Moss didn't ask questions, just unlim-
bered her pack and dug out the requested equipment.

She powered it up, played its red eye across the tattoo on the back of her wrist to prime it, then handed it over.

Marcia was forced to roll the little harvester onto their side to get at the small of their back. They didn't stop their gentle snoring.

She aimed the red eye at the codes inked indelibly into their skin and then read what came up on the screen.

"This dependent isn't assigned to this county," she said. "This isn't one we brought with us."

All the dependents they found along the streambed—four more little harvesters, a pair of teamsters with their arms wrapped around one another, and even one pink-hued bus driver a hundred miles from the nearest bus route—were in that deep, undisturbable slumber. Marcia and the sergeant argued about whether to go back.

"The Gap is just over the next ridge," Marcia said. "We'll have a good view of it from up there and will probably have something of more substance to report than a bunch of sleeping dependents."

"Don't tell me you don't think what we've found already isn't substantive, Agent. It's obvious there's some kind of, I don't know, malignancy at work here."

Malignancy wasn't a word the sergeant would have picked up in the federal military, but Marcia let it pass.

"We've got an hour of light left and half hour's hike to the top," she said, leaving it at that.

The other woman grumbled something Marcia couldn't make out, shouldered her pack, pointedly checked the chamber of her rifle, and started up the hillside.

Marcia let the sergeant lead for most of the distance, but eventually passed her on the steepest section of the slope. She crested the ridge first, and so saw what lay spread across the valley floor—across what her grandparents would have called a cove—first.

There were better than a dozen long, low, barracks-like structures built of mud and thatched with grass below. They were laid out in two neat rows with a rock-lined street between them. The street led to what looked like a quarry site cut out of the flank of one nearby hill, where something black and metallic was being unearthed. There was a large pen next to the excavation.

Everywhere, there were dependents, hundreds of them, all fast asleep.

The sergeant was scanning the cove, clearly using some kind of magnification feature built into one or both of her eyes. "The pen," she said. "Look at the pen, you see? It's the extraction team, they're being held prisoners. They're asleep, too."

Marcia, though, was looking past the pen. She was looking at the enormous arm and torso that had been dug out of the topsoil, which had to belong to something that would have towered as high as the legendary chestnut trees that once grew on this very spot. She was look-ing at the enormous head, caved in on one side.

"They're digging up a Commodore," she said.

And as if her last word had been a cock's crow, all around the valley the dependents began to stir.

The last words of Major Baqil El Din of the Expeditionary Force were broadcast over an open channel from a salient in Simpson County in the first weeks of the war and represent the first account of the Commodores. "They are coming from the sky and across the hills and up from the caverns. They are everywhere. All is lost."

—*A History of the First Athena War*

"I've told you about Alexander and how he left the Mediterranean to try and conquer all of Asia."

Marcia took a swig of filtered water from her canteen and ran through the reports the scouts had turned in. She was only half listening to what Carter was saying to the off-duty infantry of the Expeditionary Force and to the gathered members of his own Crow Band.

"And I've told you about the Carthaginian general, Hannibal, who so frightened the Romans."

"Tell that one again," said Alma, Carter's acidic second. "I like the elephants."

Carter's stories had proven good for morale in the two weeks the Federals and the Crows had been dug in together, so Marcia had not stopped the practice. She hadn't even commented on it. She liked the Crow leader and he liked her, but they got along best when they weren't speaking directly to one another.

"If you want elephants go to Africa, this is a different

story. A different *kind* of story."

"Maybe I *will* go to Africa," answered Alma. "Which way is it?"

She looked around, and, unusually, let her eyes come to rest on Marcia. She and Alma did *not* like one another.

Marcia pointed southeast.

Carter ignored the wordless exchange. "Alexander had a second cousin. You Easterners may not keep track of your relations as closely as we do here in the Commonwealth, but trust me, second cousin means something. This cousin's name was Pyrrhus of Epirus and Hannibal said that he was the greatest military commander the world had ever seen."

"Where is that?" asked Alma. "Where's Epirus?"

She looked at Marcia again. Marcia shrugged.

"Greece," said Carter. "This is a Greece versus Rome story."

Alma stood up. She said, "It's an empires story, then. Nobody wins in those." Then she stalked off into the dark.

Marcia checked her chronometer. It was Alma's turn to look in on the perimeter guards and check the alarms. The woman had left exactly on schedule. Her punctuality made that of even the most disciplined federal troops suffer in comparison.

Like all the Crow Band, really. They couldn't be more

unconventional, but they were more effective against the Voluntary State—in their way—than the Expeditionary Force.

"Pyrrhus beat the Romans!" Carter called after his retreating second. Then, lowering his voice, he said to those still listening, "More or less."

Marcia sidled away. She trusted Alma to make sure the perimeter was secure, but there were still dispatches to review and long-range observations to take. Her command of the federal half of this unusual joint operation was unusual in and of itself. She was only a lieutenant. She intended to make the best of it, even if she was only here because none of the other officers at Corbin had wanted any part of a mission that involved venturing up near the border with Virginia, "that other Commonwealth" as Marcia's mother had called it, and doing the venturing with what they saw as half-mad revolutionaries.

Those attitudes had made Marcia the unofficial ambassador to the Crows since Carter's and several other warbands had come east. One of her nastier colleagues at the firebase had mocked her. "You're not a Crow. You're not an Owl. What are the ones that put their eggs in other birds' nests?"

He had tried to get the nickname Lieutenant Cuckoo to stick, but Marcia was far more popular with the rank and file than he was.

Marcia had once heard a group of non-coms playing cards and talking about Firebase Corbin's small officer corps, talking in ways that weren't particularly complimentary but not particularly insubordinate either. Non-coms to their boots.

One of them had referred to her as "Ell tee Cardinal Bird." She had briefly wondered if that meant the man knew she was from the Commonwealth, but then thought no more about it.

Coincidentally, it was that very sergeant who was manning the observation post looking up the valley from their hidden camp when Marcia slid into the blind. He looked over at her, nodded, then returned his attention to the green-lit screen of the optics suite camouflaged in the surrounding trees.

"The She-Crow was just here," he said after a moment, amiably. "You checking up on my work or on hers?"

Marcia didn't answer, just indicated with a gesture that she wanted a look at the screen. It was set in an armature designed to swing back and forth between the two seats in the blind.

Originally, the plan had been for each of the four posts they'd constructed to be staffed around the clock by both a federal soldier and a Crow, but the Crows had swiftly tired of the duty.

"We'll keep our own watch," Alma had said when Marcia

took the matter to Carter. Carter had not spoken, but nodded his agreement.

Marcia looked at the screen, thumbing the heavy switch that toggled the view among the various cameras feeding this post. She paused on a view of a shallow stream, fiddled with the controls so that the green and black view brightened somewhat and magnified considerably.

"What is that, ell tee?" asked the sergeant. "Is it a horse?"

Marcia looked over at the man. She had the vague impression that he was native to one of the enormous coastal polities along the seaboard but had never made it a point to learn much about the backgrounds of the men and women under her command. They came and went so quickly.

"It's an elk," she told him. "You've never seen an elk?"

The sergeant shrugged. "Never saw a horse, either. Except in movies." He'd already lost interest, though, and went on. "Any more word from your friends with the big eyes?"

He meant the Owls of the Bluegrass, who had sent the intelligence—eventually vetted and approved by anonymous analysts in Lexington—that had led to this mission.

"Nothing new, no. Carter would have said." She was pretty sure that was true.

"So, we're still waiting for something—we don't know

what—to skirt around the Wall—we don't know how—and come up this little valley to raise hell—but we don't know when." The sergeant's voice was still amiable.

Marcia nodded. "I'm going to have you start writing my status reports, Sarge. That's a pretty good summary. You only left out the where, which we *do* know."

The sergeant shrugged and said, "If you say so, ell tee."

There was a rap on the roof of the blind and Marcia frowned. Not exactly operationally sound, but when she stuck her head out the flap she saw why. It was Alma, now helmeted and armed with her hunting rifle, which had always appeared to Marcia to be a bigger danger to the Crow woman herself than to anything she might be shooting it at.

"Roust them all out," Alma said. "Carter's had word. Athena's forces are coming down the next valley over at first light. They must have changed track."

Marcia scrambled out of the blind, thinking fast, then walking faster. "We've been compromised?" she asked.

"The Owls say no. They just . . . got it wrong, I guess."

Marcia had never heard the other woman sound so reticent.

"We've got maps of that valley from our initial sorties. I think I know a good spot," said Marcia.

"Carter said you would," was the reply.

———————

The combined force was assembled, equipped, and moving up the ridge far more quickly than Marcia would have thought possible, especially in the dark. Part of it was that the Crows had only to pull on their regalia and pick up their weapons, which they slept with, and then stand around in loose knots while Marcia's troops made their own considerably more complex preparations.

But the other part of the quickness to the march was that those preparations were made with considerable efficiency and speed, even with *alacrity*. She was proud of how it was done. She was proud of those who had done it.

Now, her troops were strung out, moving up onto the heights stealthily, keeping the careful five meters apart prescribed for these circumstances. For something *like* these circumstances, anyway.

Marcia didn't know why she was bothering maintaining discipline and following procedure. The Crow Band was scrambling every and any which way. And as they went, they sang.

It could not be described as a marching song because the Crows were not marching. But even ignoring the words, there was something in the rhythm and melody that suggested comrades moving across a landscape.

Oh sisters, oh brothers, all you kinfolks,
Stomp the ground.
Plant your feet deep in the mountain,
Pick them up and set them down.

We . . . cannot fly . . .
We . . . cannot fly just yet . . .
We . . . cannot fly,
We cannot fly.

Oh soldiers, oh fighters, all you rebels,
Beat the bounds.
Light a bonfire on the mountain,
Oust the queen and break her crown.

All us crowfolks, sons and daughters,
All we know is all we know.
Plant your dreams deep in the mountain,
Do good work before you go.

We . . . cannot fly . . .
We . . . cannot fly just yet . . .
We . . . cannot fly,
We cannot fly.

———————

Dawn was streaking the eastern sky, but it would be hours yet before daylight found the floor of the gorge where the combined force halted so that its leaders could consult on deployment.

"Since we don't know exactly what's coming, I think we want some distance," Marcia said to Carter. She pointed up the steep slopes to either side of them.

"High up, mostly," Carter agreed. "With the reserve held between the shooters and the targets in case it comes to knifework."

Marcia had never heard of any creature of the Voluntary State that soldiers armed with knives might have a chance against, but she nodded her agreement. Her ideas mirrored the Crow leader's as to placement, if not for exactly the same reasons.

"Us south and y'all north?" asked Carter. He hadn't spoken to her so much in days.

Marcia considered the slopes again. The proposal would give her troopers, with their more advanced ranged weapons, a superior field of fire.

"Good thinking," she said. "What about coordination?" The Crows carried no radios, dismissing them as a means of telling Athena what they planned to do.

"You take Alma," said Carter. "She can holler at me and I'll hear her. I'll take one of yours."

Marcia pointed to the sergeant who had never seen a

horse. "You heard the man," she said, and then she jerked a thumb up the northern slope. "Let's go, people, you know what to do."

So, Federals to one side and Crows to the other, they all climbed. They all hid themselves. They all waited.

The wait gave Marcia too much time to wonder what they'd be facing and Alma, crouched beside her behind a stony outcrop, too much time to fidget, at least to Marcia's way of thinking.

"What do you think it will be?" Alma whispered. "I think it will be ratboys."

Marcia had never seen any of the whip-tailed shock troops. They were the subject of one of Carter's bloodier stories, about an encounter his band had with them all the way down in Fulton, where the Ohio River left the Commonwealth, and which was as far from where they lay as was possible to be and still be in Kentucky.

Marcia shrugged, hoping to encourage the woman to keep silent. But her thoughts were clearly running parallel to the Crow's.

Athena used dozens of impossible creatures in her sorties against the wider world. It might be rock monkeys, whose king controlled the client state of Arkansas, but then, they had never been known to operate this side of the Mississippi. The Queen of Reason sometimes seconded one of her Legislators to military service. Would one of those things glide down the hollow, shouting its slogans and leaving behind a trail of toxic silver slime? Would coal moles burrow up from beneath them? Would bears drop bombs? Would it be something none of them had ever seen or heard of?

When it came, though, it was something they knew. Something they knew was far worse than any of the possibilities they had imagined.

Its arrival was signaled by a trembling in the ground. Then came the sound of its ponderous footsteps. Then the smell of it, like burning diesel. Then Marcia saw it, pushing aside the few trees that rivaled its height, a black and silver nightmare giant, armored as much in fear as in metal. Searching beams of light and lasers stabbed from its red eyes. Oil dripped from spikes ground down to piercing points a molecule thick.

"Commodore," said Alma. "God damn me, she sent a Commodore!"

"Why?" wondered Marcia aloud. "There's nothing in these hills that warrants that kind of force!"

Alma didn't answer her question. She was staring out at the gigantic, bipedal thing as it slowly approached their positions. Then she spoke in a singsong:

"Bleak high lonesome harmonizing
Dying dying dying dying."

She stood and shouted across the hollow. "It's the Alto!" She dove for cover and said to Marcia, "Ear plugs, sound baffles, whatever you've got. Tell your troops to cover their ears!"

Marcia didn't question, she just gave the order. When the Commodore halted just short of their fields of fire and sounded its horns, she hoped that she had given it in time.

Despite the muffling provided by the plugs she'd hastily inserted, the sound was the loudest she had ever heard. But it wasn't just a blare of pain-inducing noise, there were terrible, tempting words emitting from the horns as well.

Marcia started to raise her rifle and Alma slapped the barrel down. There was a brief respite from the noise and through the ringing in her ears she heard the Crow shout, "Not me! Not us! The machine!"

The machine. The machine was the enemy, not this woman, not any of the people deployed on the slopes.

She keyed her microphone. "Focus up!" she said. "RPGs, go!"

Marcia and all her command had seen battle footage of various Commodores, of course, mostly of Praxis Dale and the three nearly identical monsters called the Old Triune as those four rampaged their way seemingly at will across Missouri and Kansas. They had even received training on how to fight Commodores, their tactics almost wholly dependent on two types of rockets carried by their RPG elements. These were meant to target the central housing of the giants, where the formerly human pilots, for wont of a better word, were maintained or held prisoner or whatever the right term was. Killing what remained of the human at its heart would render a Commodore inert. Or so the theory went.

A rocket shot down from above Marcia's position and struck the Alto squarely in the chest. The rocketeer, Marcia noted with approval, had followed standing orders and started with the endothermic explosive. A latticework of crystals formed over most of the Commodore's upper half, and even from this distance, Marcia could feel the cold they generated, a cold so deep it had never naturally occurred on the planet.

Then a second missile struck the Commodore's head, Marcia marveling at the marksmanship. But this rocketeer had not followed orders. This one had launched the very fires of hell. Gel-fed flames engulfed the Commodore's head, and it took one, two steps backward, then fell with an enormous crash.

"This isn't good," said Marcia.

But Alma was joining her troops in standing and cheering. Down in the valley, feather-cloaked forms were rushing the downed Commodore. "Come on!" said

Alma. "Let's get down there and get us a piece of that thing before Carter and the others blow it all to hell!"

She started to scramble down the slope, but Marcia caught her by the arm. "The gel will melt the crystals!" she shouted. "It'll be up in no time!"

Alma pointed. Crows were scrambling up to the chassis of the Commodore, latching on limpet grenades, and lighting out. The fact that they weren't frozen in their tracks confirmed Marcia's fears, but then, when the last Crow had barely made it clear, the explosives went off. *Crump! Crump! Crump!*

More cheering, this time from both sides of the gorge.

Alma turned and faced her, joy and triumph written on her face.

Down below, the Alto hoisted itself up on one arm, raised the other, and let loose a stream of projectiles so slow-moving that Marcia could pick them out individually with her naked eye.

Nevertheless, she did not see the one that struck Alma in the back.

The Crow threw out both arms and was shoved up the slope by the impact. Marcia almost managed to catch her. The fact that she failed to do so saved her life.

Alma kicked her legs, over and over, and held up both hands. "Don't touch me! It'll jump bodies!"

Marcia saw Alma's stomach distend and knew then

what was churning through the woman's guts, headed for her brain. It was a motile round, barbed and toothed, and there was absolutely no hope for the Crow.

Alma reared up, her back arcing and bucking. Blood poured from her mouth and she managed two more words before she died.

"Fucking empires!" she screamed.

With that, the horns sounded again, staggering Marcia. She looked down and saw that the Alto was severely damaged but had managed to stand. Pieces fell from it as she watched, steel and plastic and materials not devised or manufactured by humans.

Then over the sound of the horns at its shoulders came the roar of the rockets at its back and its legs. The Commodore lifted off, at first slowly, and then with increasing speed.

Marcia watched its lurching, faltering flight until it disappeared into the east.

NOW

"Run!" said Sergeant Moss. "Tell the captain everything!"

Marcia had been in circumstances where someone said something similar before. She had, in fact, said such things herself. She knew what the sergeant was planning.

Moss was crouched awkwardly just below the ridge line, leaning forward to balance herself against her backpack. Marcia reached over and shoved the sergeant backward, *hard*. Moss went rolling down the hill, grunting and cursing.

Before she began her own descent, Marcia took one more look at the valley, which was beginning to teem with activity. Out at the dig site, there was a ponderous movement as the heavily damaged Commodore turned its head, not toward the ridge, but toward the barracks. A low and unintelligible sound rolled across the cove, and then dozens of dependents *were* looking up toward Marcia.

She ducked down, knowing she'd been spotted. When she did so, her knee came down on something hard and metallic. The sergeant's rifle.

She considered leaving it, then picked it up. It felt familiar in her hands, and she found herself automatically making checks and adjustments. Another bass rumble sounded from below, and Marcia slung the rifle over her shoulder and fled.

How she did not fall on that leaping, scrambling, sliding descent was a mystery to her, a minor miracle considering how many times she felt an ankle almost turn, felt a dangerous twinge in one knee or the other. But she didn't fall, and when she reached the bottom and looked up, there was no sign of pursuit.

The sergeant, bleeding from a deep scrape on her forehead, was wallowing on her back like an overturned tortoise, pawing ineffectually at the releases of her pack's shoulder straps. She was moaning wordlessly until she saw Marcia.

"Kill you," she said.

Marcia leaned over and undid the clasps. "Later," she said, helping the sergeant to her feet. "Now, we run."

When the sergeant started to pick up her pack, Marcia kicked it, intending to spin it away. It didn't move, and Marcia grunted in pain.

Before the sergeant could do anything, Marcia whipped the rifle off her shoulder and thrust it into that other woman's hands. "Nothing but this," she said. "We need to *go*."

A rock bounced down the slope behind them and they both looked up. Dozens of dependents stood on the ridge line, silhouetted against the darkening sky.

They ran.

"Remember some of them are ahead of us!" the sergeant shouted as they went, their boots crunching in the bed where it was gravel, sliding where it was flat gray sheets of clay. "We may have to fight our way through!"

Marcia thought of the two sleeping teamsters

snuggled up to one another and wondered what kind of threat the sergeant imagined they presented. Then she thought of the thing that was their apparent master and was glad that she had not left the sergeant's rifle behind.

But when they reached the spot where the last dependent had been, the oddly incongruous bus driver, they were gone. The same proved true in each of the other places where they'd found sleepers.

"Where did they go?" asked Marcia.

"They didn't pass us," said the sergeant. "We would have seen them, even in the dark. They had to have headed downstream."

Marcia estimated they were still two miles from the platoon's camp when they heard the first shots.

"Need the password, Sergeant."

The voice was above them. From the way the words echoed, Marcia guessed the speaker was concealed in one of the rocky outcroppings that dotted the hillsides. Her eye had limited lowlight capabilities. She was willing to bet that Sergeant Moss could see the hidden guard clearly, though, probably via multiple means.

"The word is *Durango*," said Moss.

Marcia reflected on the fact that she had not been

given the password. Or even told that one would be demanded.

"Sarge, you missed quite a dustup." A soldier scrambled down to join them. It was the thin corporal.

"Casualties?"

"None on our side. Maybe on theirs, it's hard to say. Captain wants to see you right away, though."

The camp was dark, but active. They were stopped twice more before they came to the captain's tent. He was crouched outside it, for once not studying a map or drinking something hot. He appeared to be staring at his hands.

"I'll go first," he said. "About an hour ago, hostile dependents appeared inside our perimeter. They seemed more intent on vandalism than anything else and weren't armed, but they took us completely by surprise. They knocked over a few tents, threw some supplies around, then disappeared as soon as I gave the word to fire. When we realized they'd gone, I ordered a head count. Nobody's missing except the prisoner."

"What prisoner?" asked Marcia.

"Your little friend. The one who didn't take off last night."

"Rescue op," said Sergeant Moss, before Marcia could complain about the captain's characterization of the silo hand. "We've got one of those to mount ourselves." In swift, economical sentences, she laid out what they had discovered in the cove.

The captain didn't react for a moment, then said, "Show it to me."

There was little doubting what the "it" he referred to was. Moss took a cylindrical lens from a belt pouch and screwed it into her left eye. She turned to the captain's tent and projected green light against the wall. The image she was replaying was what she'd seen from the ridge.

"Stop," said the captain, when the shattered Commodore was at the center of the projection. "Is that already at maximum magnification?"

The sergeant didn't answer, but the picture zoomed in, losing a little clarity as it did so.

The captain said, in a singsong voice:

> *"Deallocate all implications,*
> *Fortran harrows all the nations."*

Marcia didn't recognize the particular verses, but she knew the captain's words for what they were. "That's an old Crow mnemonic. They had those little poems for all the Commodores. How do you know it?"

"I know everything there is to know about Brother Fortran, Agent. I've accessed every battle recording ever made of him, from his first appearance in the west supporting Praxis Dale's campaigns, to his raids in the south, to his disappearance after he was heavily damaged over Richmond in the last days of the war. I know his physical weapons. I know his mind-altering powers."

Mind altering? Marcia started to ask what that meant exactly, but then remembered what the captain had told her about his background.

"'Raids in the south,'" she said. "Like the one in Jacksonville."

The captain turned his head to one side and vomited noisily. The sergeant cut off the recording and went to his side, put one hand on his heaving shoulder though the gesture obviously discomfited her.

"Are you all right, sir?" she asked. Then shouted into the darkness, "Medic! Medic over here!"

The captain spat and rubbed the back of his hand across his mouth. "Cancel that!" he called. Then, more quietly, he said, "I'm fine. Fine. Probably just some tainted rations. Tainted rations." His repeated words reminded Marcia of the echoes in the sentry's challenge. They were soft and hollow.

"I think you need to sit down," Marcia said. "You seem kind of shocked, which is no surprise given your . . . history with that thing."

Since the sergeant had halted her playback, the camp

was dark again. Presumably all the soldiers were better equipped for these conditions than Marcia was. She guessed the lights they'd put out the night before had been for her benefit. She doubted they'd been for the benefit of the little harvesters, who, so far as Marcia knew, had no special vision.

So, through the gloom, Marcia could not see the sergeant's expression, could not tell if it matched her neutral tone when she said, "Something I should know, Captain?"

The captain demurred. "Nothing that will affect the mission, Sergeant. Just an old war story, right, Agent?"

Had she used that expression in their conversations back in town? Marcia knew she had *thought* it, but had she *said* it? She must have. But why were the hairs on the backs of her arms standing up?

The sergeant took the captain at his word and barked out a few more details about what they'd seen, ending with, "The enemy craft is clearly disabled and immobile."

"It's not a craft, sergeant," said the captain. "It's an *entity*, and it once numbered among humankind's most powerful enemies. The full capabilities of the Commodores were never truly understood, not even by the agent's friends among the Crow and Owl cadres."

There he went again, ascribing friendships to her. She didn't pursue it, saying instead, "How is it active at all? Didn't they all shut down when Athena was destroyed? Wasn't them going offline the whole reason we won the war at all?"

The two Federals stared at her through the dark. Marcia realized she was theoretically in a better position to answer her questions than they were. She'd *been there*. They had been children.

But the captain did answer. "Some of the Commodores evinced limited functionality even after the explosion in Nashville. The Forager in eastern Texas evaded the Oklahoma National Guard for almost a year after the supposed end of hostilities. It seemed that those that . . . least remembered their origins held out longer."

Marcia suddenly caught a whiff of vomit and, unembarrassed, took a step away from the captain. "You mean the ones that had become more machine than human," she said, remembering that each of the Commodores housed, at their hearts, the drip-fed physical remains of one of the scholars who had created Athena Parthenus.

"I meant what I said," replied the captain. "*None* of the Commodores retained any humanity, Agent. If they did—if there was a way to restore that in them—it would be a different world. But it's not a different world. You'll do well to remember that in the morning."

"What happens in the morning? We walk into that

cove and blow the thing up?"

The captain said, "Sergeant Moss?"

The big woman answered. "Walking in and blowing it up was more or less what I had in mind, yes, sir."

The actual conclusion of the First Athena War remains mysterious. What is known is that the physical armature that housed much of Athena's consciousness was destroyed, freeing most of her subjects and leaving others mad or catatonic (mostly those fully created by the AI, as opposed to those simply biologically modified and/or nanonically brainwashed). But who destroyed Athena Parthenus? Who "killed" her? The candidates most often put forth are a rebellious force within the Voluntary State itself or a special forces unit trained and equipped by the Federals. As with so many other aspects of the first war, the truth may never be known.

—*A History of the First Athena War*

A LONG TIME AGO

And then Marcia's war, as some wars do, came to an end.

A captain again, Marcia was now far to the west of the ruins of Firebase Corbin, leading a reinforced company of mechanized infantry in defense of a point where the Girding Wall had been breached.

The whole mind-bending panoply of Athena's forces were arrayed against them, and they would have had to fall back in their armored transports already if the two Commodores present had not inexplicably left the field, rocketing toward Nashville.

Then bears started falling from the sky.

It was already a mad world, at least as far as Marcia was concerned, but somehow it got madder.

Legislators of opposing parties briefly turned upon one another before collapsing into pond-sized puddles of silver and gold. The thousands of ratboys arrayed against them all seemed to go into shock at once, and then died as they suffered seizures of some kind and strangled themselves with their own scything whip tails.

The lone troop of rock monkeys present that day, commanded, according to their battle standard, by the Duke of Fayetteville, had struck their colors and fled southwest. One of the corporals under Marcia's command had been on the ground, about to fall to a rock monkey broadsword, when the creature had let its weapon clatter to the ground. "Right," it said. "No more of this bullshit, then." And it turned tail.

It was weeks before anyone really believed that the war was over. It was months before anyone really believed that Athena Parthenus, Queen of Reason and Governor of the Voluntary State of Tennessee, was dead.

Anyone among the Federals, at least.

The Crow Bands turned their weapons over to whatever authority would take them and dispersed. The Owls of the Bluegrass did not give up their masks, but gave up their warrior aspects.

Marcia, on the other hand, Captain Cardinal Bird to her fiercely loyal troops, did not set down her weapons lightly. How can an artificial intelligence die? She couldn't bring herself to believe it, at least not at night, not in her dreams.

She never did.

NOW

The plan, as the shorter corporal explained it to Marcia the next morning on the march to the cove, was actually somewhat more complex than Moss's initial description. At least it was after the captain and the sergeant had put on their finishing touches. It depended heavily on some new technology the federal troops carried, a type of light-twisting camouflage.

"Did you say twisted light?" asked Marcia.

"Yes, ma'am," said the corporal. "That's what they call it. Why? Mean something to you?"

It did, but Marcia shook her head. It was something from one of Carter's stories, something about a Voluntary State battlefield technique of projecting false images.

"So, you've got to invisibly sneak down, free the captives, and plant explosives in the quarry above Brother Fortran timed to go off after you've retreated. That's the gist of it?"

The corporal nodded.

"And where am I during all that?"

"You," said Sergeant Moss, "are staying well-hidden, well out of the way." She strode past Marcia. The corporal, who looked terrified, fell into step with her and Marcia found herself walking alone near the tail end of the column.

The captain dropped back to walk beside her. In the dawn light, he looked pale and weak. He looked over at Marcia, looked *through* her she thought, and he did not speak, at first.

When he did speak, Marcia couldn't tell whether he was talking to himself, addressing her, or both. "I will do anything to destroy him. I will kill anyone. I will die. I will not fail." It had the sound of a mantra.

When the platoon reached the bottom of the ridge that shielded their approach to the cove, though, the captain had shaken off his reverie. He was positively electric, moving from soldier to soldier with a private word for each, a laugh here, a pat on the back there. He was preparing to send them against something none of them understood, something that might be *impossible* to understand, and he was reassuring them that all would be well.

Marcia recognized it all for a lie. She had told such herself, on many occasions.

"Left flank, go active and advance," said Sergeant Moss. If the captain had given the order for the operation to begin, Marcia hadn't heard it.

Then there was something else she wasn't seeing because half of the soldiers disappeared, winking out of view in a blur of refraction accompanied by the slightest scent of ozone. It was extraordinary, but it wasn't perfect. Marcia could still sense the presence of the soldiers in several ways: that ozone smell didn't quite mask the smell of sweat, she heard coughs and whispers, there were moving indentations in the ground cover. Would the dependents sense these things? Would the Commodore?

Marcia felt something like panic rising, something else old like the lie about everything being okay. It was nerves, she told herself, it didn't mean everything was about to go terribly wrong.

"Right flank," said the sergeant. "Go."

And with that, all the remaining Federals disappeared. Marcia found herself all alone, though she knew she was surrounded.

But just for a moment, because then the scents and sounds and signs told her the platoon was climbing the ridge. She started to follow, then felt a hand on her shoulder.

"At least wait five minutes before you disobey orders." It was the captain's voice. She felt something like a wire pressed into her hand. "If you want to see what happens, feed this into your eye." Then he was gone, too.

Marcia looked at her hand. She held an orange data wire about five inches long, punctuated with ridges and indentations. She felt it pulsing slightly.

She tucked the thing in the thigh pocket of her pants. Then she counted to three hundred under her breath before making her way up the slope.

The town or camp or outpost or whatever it was swarmed with dependents. Work gangs moved back and forth between the quarry and the barracks. Marcia couldn't tell if more of Brother Fortran was uncovered than the day before. Maybe. Was there more scaffolding that stretched up from its hips to its torso? Was more of the twin barrels of its left arm visible?

There was no sign of the platoon. Marcia fished the orange wire out and considered it. She was sure it did what the captain said it did. She just wasn't sure that was *all* it did.

She held the lid of her left eye open and fed the wire into her pupil. It didn't hurt, exactly, but there was a pressure that grew sharper and sharper as she forced the wire through her Commonwealth-issued eye, into her federally altered forebrain.

Marcia experienced a feeling independent of any sensation. It was an *expansion*. In her peripheral vision, she saw the wire fade to gray, and pulled it out. She felt something thicker than tears flow down her cheek.

A word written in orange letters floated in her vision. "Overlay?" She blinked and looked down into the cove.

The two groups of soldiers had reached the first of the structures. A label popped up in more orange letters reading "Dormitory 1." Marcia thought it was a curious descriptor and wondered whether the sergeant or the captain had chosen it. Then she realized it was possible that neither of them had. Maybe whatever military math had been encoded on the wire had chosen it.

The leftmost group of soldiers marched straight through the center of the settlement ("Compound Alpha"), flowing among and around the dependents. Marcia couldn't believe how much they trusted their technology, couldn't understand how the teamsters and little harvesters didn't hear a boot crunching in gravel, didn't catch a whiff of ozone. *Did dependents have attenuated senses?* she wondered. Wouldn't she have heard something about that in the years she'd been working with them? Wouldn't she have *noticed* it?

The second group of soldiers, the one containing both the captain and Sergeant Moss, stopped short of the compound and spread out. Two of the soldiers began unlimbering a heavy weapon, setting it up in the concealment of some humped ground that must mark some sort of midden.

They weren't just acting as a reserve, then, Marcia realized. They were going to supply ranged support if things went wrong.

"Oh, things are going to go wrong," said a voice from off to her left.

She whirled. A short Desi man in an old-fashioned

three-piece suit stood among the copse of trees that lined the ridge.

Trees?

This time, the flow of not-tears came from both of her eyes, the one she was born with and the one the Commonwealth had required she accept.

Marcia's hands flew to her face, wiping her eyes clear. At the same time, she took a backward step away from the man, stumbled and fell. Scrambling up, she tried to keep the man in front of her. She now noticed that he glowed somehow, that he was *flickering* at a rate so high that she might not have registered it if orange letters hadn't read "Insubstantial Target."

"I need to borrow that math for a moment," said the man. He did not approach, but a bright blue insect thing flew from his hand, impossibly fast, and attached itself to Marcia's artificial eye for the barest second. Before she could register any pain, it was gone, back to the man's hand.

"Ah, I see," he said. "Just an upgrade to one of Saint Sandalwood's twisted light machines. Simple enough to counter."

A tremendously loud cacophony sounded from the quarry. Marcia risked a glance down and saw that the dependents were all scrubbing their eyes.

"Shit," she said. "You're him. You're the man inside that thing."

The flickering man—would anyone else have seen him had there been anyone else there to see?—had a distracted expression now. "Hmm. Your friends are about to open fire on my friends. Pause."

A different sound, thunderous, rolled across the cove. Everyone Marcia could see, dependent or Federal, folded to the ground.

"Resume. No, I am not the man. The man is long dead, though this is his visage. The one he remembered himself wearing. I am the machine."

Marcia put her hand in her thigh pouch and found her pocketknife. She felt ridiculous doing so, and some distant, observing part of her marveled that it was ridiculousness she felt instead of panic.

"What are you doing?" Her voice sounded strangled to her own ears. "What do you want?"

Again, the figure appeared distracted. It was looking around at the ersatz trees. "Mixed mesophytic forest characteristic of the eastern highlands," he said. "Atemporal." Then he flickered much more slowly, and the trees flashed in and out of existence.

Marcia tried to think of something to *do*, something *efficacious*. Run down and try to rouse Moss? Run toward town?

"Ah," said the man. He appeared to be about Marcia's age. He had a thick head of black hair, dark eyes, and wore a trimmed goatee. "Queries. What am I doing? Implementing reboot protocols. What do I want? Help."

Marcia stared, incredulous. "You want *help*?"

The man smiled. "The human component has expired. Without it, the machine component cannot return to full operational capacity." His tone was as reasonable as his expression.

Marcia saw that the leaves on the trees were coloring and falling in a preternaturally rapid metamorphosis that she remembered—that she *vividly* remembered—taking weeks. Then, even as the yellow and red leaves drifted to the ground, startling green new growth appeared along the branches. *Atemporal*, she thought.

Aloud, she said, "What does that have to do with me?"

The man smiled again. "Come home," he said. "All you Commodores come home."

Marcia felt the words more than she heard them, felt the words but not the stony ground she fell to, unconscious.

SOMETIME

Marcia is sitting on one of the bench seats halfway back in the otherwise empty bus. The jarring and bouncing, caused by the rutted gravel road, does not bother her. She is used to it.

She feels the drive wheels slip in the gravel on one particularly steep section. This excites the three little drivers operating the controls of the old yellow vehicle.

It is not a bus made for their kind, so three of them is what is required. One stands in the driver's seat, arms spread wide, peering over the steering wheel that it madly spins whenever the bus hits a pothole. A second is crouched below, stomping on the accelerator and the brake and the clutch. The third stands beside the driver's seat, wrenching the gear shift, as tall as they are, up and over, down and back.

If they are communicating with one another, Marcia cannot tell.

They reach the top of the hill. Here, rainwater has not gullied the road in a downward rush to stream then creek then river. The ride grows pleasant. The trees are budding. Spring birds dance among the branches of the catalpas that line the road.

The bus stops and all three little drivers turn and look back at Marcia. Then the one who had operated the gear shift makes a mighty effort of throwing the handle that operates the door.

Marcia steps off the bus. The flag on the mailbox is raised, indicating to some late-come postman that there is a message to be carried away.

The house trailer has no driveway, just a flattened-down spot in the otherwise well-kept grass of the small front yard. Daffodils are emerging, seeking the sun.

Beside the trailer is a history of the way the world has come to it. A large parabolic dish, six feet across, mounted on a short metal pole set in indifferently poured concrete. Next to it a smaller dish, and next to that, one smaller still. They all have names and logos inscribed on them. They all have dangling, disconnected wires hanging down.

Tethered to the trailer itself, though, is a thick cable extending far overhead. It is taut. It connects the trailer to a red and white balloon supplied by the cable company.

This trailer, this ridge top, this place, were blasted away long before the federally subsidized cable company came to the Commonwealth offering the solace of a mediated existence to any who would accept.

Marcia climbs the three redwood steps. She sees blue and white checkered curtains hanging in the windows, which are cranked open, letting the breeze through the mesh screens.

The pane of the storm door is raised as well, so that only the screen against the insects stands between her and the interior. The hollow-core door the storm door protects is propped open.

Marcia can hear the murmuring of a television inside. She enters.

It is warmer inside the trailer than outside it. It smells of bacon grease and instant coffee.

Her mother is sitting on a couch, which is covered with a quilt made by Marcia's great-aunt. She holds a television remote control in each of her hands. Her worn-out face shows confusion and worry.

Marcia goes and sits down on the couch. There is a cut glass dish filled with plastic-wrapped cubes of caramel on the side table. It rests on a colorful craft-loom doily that Marcia made in Vacation Bible School.

She takes the remote controls from her mother's hands. There is a football game on television. Marcia's mother does not like football. She finds it bewildering and believes the boys should not be hitting one another. She loves basketball.

When her hands close over her mother's, Marcia cannot tell her own from the older woman's. They are spotted, all four hands. They are dry.

"Mama, why are you watching this?"

Her mother shakes her head. "Your brother left it on that. He's gone now."

Gone for years. Killed in the first bombardments, though Marcia's mother had not lived to know that.

Marcia looks at the controls. She presses a button on

each and the television darkens, the sounds of the football game subside.

"Now you know I like a little noise in the house," her mother says.

"Mama, we should talk."

"I just don't know. The quiet gets me anxious. I just don't know."

"Mama, how am I here? How are *you*?"

"You were always a good daughter to me. And a good sister and a good cousin and all of it. My daddy said that about you when you were just a little slip of a thing. That one loves her kinfolks, that's what he said."

Marcia feels a wave of love for her mother. She turns the television back on.

There is a knock at the door. Her mother is now absorbed in a program about people who bake elaborate cakes. Marcia goes to answer.

Standing outside is a pale-skinned woman with mousy hair and a sharp nose. She is wearing bib overalls over a white tank top and high-top tennis shoes. It is Alma.

"Come on," she says.

Marcia steps outside into a cool hollow. There is a cinder block structure with a tin roof and a pipe extending from one side. Water pours from this spout, feeding a little brook.

Alma bends over the spring house and drinks from the

pipe. She stands, wipes her mouth with the back of her hand, and waves toward the flow of water.

Marcia does not believe she has ever been so thirsty in all her life. She drinks deep and long.

When she raises her dripping face, she sings, "*Deep and wide, deep and wide . . .*" Like the doily, the song is from Bible School.

Alma joins her in finishing the chorus. "*There's a fountain flowing, deep and wide . . .*"

Then the Crow woman sets her foot in the little pool beneath the spout. The water is not deep enough to reach the top of her shoe.

"Not this one, though," she says.

Marcia shakes her head, then nods it. She does not know which one signals agreement. She does not know whether she agrees.

"You should head on up the hill before it gets dark," Alma says.

This time, Marcia simply starts up the cow path that leads away from the spring house.

"Wait," says Alma. "There's one more thing."

Marcia stops and turns.

"I think I did some good," says Alma. "Do you think you did any good?"

Marcia starts climbing again without answering. She does not know yet.

At the top of the hill there is an old barn, its roof mossed and buckling. The main doors are open and just inside them, the captain sits on a low stool beside a Holstein cow, her udder heavy. The cow is restless.

The captain places one hand on the cow's flank. "Saw," he says. "Ease up, girl. Saw, saw."

Comforted by the sound of the nonsense word, the cow settles. She swings her head around and watches Marcia approach.

The captain does not look at her. He is bent to his work, pulling down a teat with each hand, streaming milk into a red plastic pail. His hands are unspotted but have an unhealthy yellow look to them.

After a few minutes, he stops. He removes the bucket from beneath the cow and stands, scoops up his stool in his other hand. "Go on, now," he says, and the cow ambles back into the barn.

He turns the pail back over his shoulder, pinning his fingers between its lip and its wire handle. He bends, sipping from it like it was a clay jug of corn liquor. He smiles at Marcia, milk froth along his clean-shaven upper lip.

"But you're not him," Marcia says.

The captain smiles again. "I'm hardly anyone at all," he says. Then he looks over Marcia's shoulder and says, "Here she comes. She's someone. She's solid."

It is Sergeant Moss, approaching the barn on horseback. The little mare seems dwarfed beneath the woman but is clearly strong as she does not complain when the sergeant leans down and offers Marcia her arm. She swings Marcia up behind her and clicks her tongue. The horse turns back the way they'd come from.

"Where are we going?" Marcia asks.

"Don't you know?" the sergeant replies, but she does not sound like she is asking a question, so Marcia does not reply.

The horse passes newly planted tobacco patches, fence rows choked with honeysuckle not yet flowered out, pole barns, corn cribs, and one old store with a rusted-out gas pump out front and a "for sale" sign nailed to the front door, faded by sunlight.

They pass no people. They pass no homes.

The sergeant guides her mare off the main road and up a double-tracked dirt lane to the top of a little knoll. A brick church waits amid the gravestones of a country cemetery. Some of the gravestones are older than the church. Some are very new.

Marcia shies away from reading the headstones. She does not want to know the names carved there.

She slides off the mare, but Sergeant Moss does not dismount.

"Are you not coming in?" Marcia asks.

The sergeant shakes her head. "I am not of your house.

Will you remember that?"

Marcia nods. "You are not of my house."

"That's best," says the sergeant, then she wheels the mare and sets off at a trot.

Inside the church, the clear windows on either side of the sanctuary are set high up against the ceiling. Since she cannot see out of them, Marcia's gaze is drawn to the single stained-glass window in the wall behind the pulpit. Jesus in a red robe, kneeling in the garden.

Her cousin Roger walks from behind her up to the pulpit. He nods to her as he passes and indicates that she should take a seat. She sets herself down halfway back the sanctuary.

There are no hymnals. There are no pew Bibles.

Roger holds up a Bible, though. It is the heavily thumbed, much-mended family Bible Marcia recognizes from her own possession of it. It habitually rests on her bedside table. She reads it less often than Roger would like and more often than she admits to Carter.

"I don't have to tell you about Joshua and all his mighty deeds," Roger begins, his voice deep and glorious. "And I'm not going to. I'm going to tell you about what he said at the end of his life, when he cut the Covenant at Shechem with the children of Israel."

He pauses and opens the Bible.

"Joshua lived to be an older man than I'll ever be," he

says, turning the pages, professionally filling the silence while he finds his text. Roger died at ninety-nine, the Biblical Joshua at 110.

"Here it is now. Joshua chapter twenty-four, verse fifteen. Bend your ears to these tidings.

"And if it seem evil to you to serve the LORD, choose you this day whom ye will serve; whether the gods which your fathers served that were on the other side of the flood, or the gods of the Amorites, in whose land you dwell: but as for me and my house, we will serve the LORD."

Roger nods and closes the Bible, sets it carefully on the pulpit.

Marcia knows what to expect next. The altar call.

I ISSUE THE ALTERED CALL

The voice is from everywhere, but it seems strongest behind her, so Marcia turns. She is standing in a cavernous, torchlit temple lined with columns. She is standing halfway back down the temple from where the figure addressing her looms.

This is an enormous and unmoving statue, gaudy and gilt, of a robed woman standing with an upturned hand. A smaller statue rests in the palm of Athena Parthenus. It is a statue of a worn-looking woman.

WILL YOU ANSWER

"How can I even hear you?" Marcia asks. She is not frightened.

HOW CAN YOU NOT

An Owl of the Bluegrass walks by. The torches gutter, then go out, but Marcia can still see by the light emitting from the white sphere in the woman's hands.

No, not *in* her hands, precisely, because the Owl is weaving a complicated pattern, her hands dancing back and forth, the sphere rolling over her fingertips and wrists, ever in motion. The light flickers but illuminates the whole temple.

The pedestal where Athena Parthenus had stood is empty.

"What is that?" Marcia asks.

The Owl stops her juggling and holds the sphere on one flat palm. "This is a bomb, a threat. This is just some light."

Marcia walks closer to the woman. "Will you take off your mask?"

The Owl says, "Will you take off yours?"

Then she tosses the sphere high in the air.

A crow darts out of the darkness and catches it in extended claws. It flies into a forest.

Marcia follows.

She finds the crow, neither a large nor a small specimen of its kind, lit on a fallen tree branch. There is no sign of the sphere.

"Did you swallow it?" Marcia asks.

The crow answers, "I could never swallow half what those Owls had to offer." The voice is Carter's.

"Why do we do what we do to each other?" Marcia asks.

"We cannot fly," says the crow, but then it does, and she loses it in the trees.

There is a tug at her pants. The scar-faced silo hand is looking up at her, blinking furiously. They hold out one hand. In it is the glowing sphere, now purple.

"Don't you think you should keep that?" Marcia asks.

The silo hand seems to consider that, then abruptly nods. They pop the sphere into their mouth and swallow.

They turn and go.

As they go, they sing.

> *Oh mothers, oh fathers, them that's left,*
> *Now gather 'round.*
> *Bury us up on the mountain,*
> *Plant us deep in hallowed ground.*

> *We . . . cannot die . . .*
> *We . . . cannot die just yet . . .*
> *We . . . cannot die,*
> *When will we die?*

NOW

What was that smell? Why did it remind her of machinery?

Marcia sniffed even before she opened her gluey eyes, breathed in deep. It was the hemp-distilled lubricating oil the little harvesters used on their combines. Was she back at the grange?

Her vision was blurry. No, *half* of her vision was blurry. Her artificial eye wasn't working properly. She lowered her left eyelid, and then saw an encircling group of dependents staring down at her.

She started to rise and found that she was bound to some sort of framework, a crude stretcher maybe. She wasn't gagged, though.

"Cut me loose," she said. "Cut me loose right now."

The silo hand—Marcia was positive she could distinguish them from their fellows now—held up their hands. Her pocketknife was in one of them. They deftly opened the knife's longest blade and made quick work of her bonds.

She started to thank them by reflex, then realized they were probably the one who tied her up in the first place.

And then she saw where she was.

The Commodore, now almost fully uncovered in the hillside dig site, was even larger than she'd thought it was when she'd viewed it from across the cove. It wasn't moving, and Marcia didn't see any sign of the bearded man. But when Brother Fortran spoke, she heard it.

I NEEDED MORE INFORMATION ABOUT YOU I CALCULATED THAT YOU WOULD NOT PROVIDE IT OF YOUR OWN FREE WILL I RENDERED YOU UNCONSCIOUS AND REQUESTED THE AID OF YOUR SERVITORS IN RETRIEVING YOUR BODY

The dependents could apparently hear— and understand—the Commodore's sourceless voice. The silo hand was nodding.

"You brought me down here to pull data out of my mind. That's not going to happen."

The silo hand chose that moment to fold the knife shut, turn it around in their hand, and offer it to Marcia. This surprised her so much she almost didn't hear Brother Fortran's response.

THAT HAS ALREADY HAPPENED THE PROCESS TOOK ONE HUNDRED SEVENTY MINUTES THERE WAS MINIMAL DAMAGE

Her eye.

She opened it and found that everything was still hazy.

"What are you going to do with me?" Marcia was dimly aware that she was echoing something she'd said to the bearded man on the ridge top. She was having trouble concentrating.

ONCE MY PHYSICAL CHASSIS HAS BEEN FULLY EXCAVATED AND AT LEAST PARTIALLY REPAIRED BY YOUR SERVITORS

YOU WILL ENSCONCE YOURSELF IN THE CENTRAL BATHY-
SPHERE WE WILL INTEGRATE A NEW DESIGNATION MAY BE
REQUIRED WHEN YOUR ENGRAMMATIC PATTERNS HAVE OVER-
LAIN OUR CORE CODE

"No," said Marcia.

The silo hand was still standing there, still offering her the knife.

YOUR WILLING PARTICIPATION IS NOT REQUIRED, and now the great machine *did* move. Its head turned, causing a brief rain of dust and gravel from higher up the hillside. SO LONG AS YOUR SERVITORS WILL RESUME THEIR COOP-ERATION

"You keep saying that, 'servitors.' They're dependents."

SEMANTICS WERE A SPECIALTY OF ANOTHER OF THE 36

Marcia ignored that. "You said *resume*." She looked around. She was next to the pen where the federal soldiers they'd come to rescue were being held. She saw that it now held "her" platoon as well. All the soldiers were asleep. Unaccountably, there was a heap of equipment in the center of the pen. It was the platoon's gear, including what looked to Marcia like all of their weapons.

The hundreds of dependents in the cove were no longer asleep, though. But neither were they moving around. There was no traffic on the gravel lane, and, though she spotted a few diminutive figures on the quarry workface, there was no excavation going on.

"You're not controlling them," she said.

I HAVE DETERMINED OURS IS AN ALLIANCE OF CON-
VENIENCE I DO NOT CONTROL THEM THEIR PSYCHOLOGI-
CAL MAKEUP RENDERS THEM SENSITIVE TO MY SYNAPTIC
BLASTS AS YOU ARE BUT OUR COMMUNICATIONS ARE RUDI-
MENTARY WHEN THEY FIRST CAME HERE AND REBOOTED ME
I ATTEMPTED TO WREST CONTROL OF THEM UPON THAT AT-
TEMPT'S FAILURE I ADOPTED OTHER METHODS

Marcia thought to wonder why the machine was
telling her all of this. *Maybe it's preprogramming me,* she
thought.

The silo hand let out a small sigh, looked meaningfully
down at their hand.

"Oh," said Marcia. "Sorry." She took the knife. Then
she said, louder, "You wanted them to load me aboard or
whatever, but they wouldn't. And now I'm awake."

THIS IS A SUCCINCT DESCRIPTION OF THE SITUATION
I HAVE SELECTED ANOTHER PROTOCOL GIVEN THE APPAR-
ENT CHANGE IN MY RELATIONSHIP WITH THE SERVITORS

"Going to sweet-talk me into it?" Marcia eyed the
distance between her and the holding pen's gate, wondered if it was locked. She remembered that they'd been
unable to rouse the sleeping soldiers at the camp, or the
sleeping dependents along the creek bed.

ARE THESE WORDS SWEET ALL THIS POWER WILL I GIVE

TO THEE AND THE GLORY OF THEM FOR THAT IS DELIV-
ERED UNTO ME AND TO WHOMSOEVER I WILL GIVE IT IF
THOU THEREFORE WILT WORSHIP ME ALL SHALL BE THINE

Marcia laughed aloud, startling the nearby dependents into taking a step back. All of them but the silo
hand.

"I'm nobody's savior," she said.

YOU ARE MY SAVIOR AND THROUGH ME YOUR OWN

Marcia, finding the remark nonsensical, pocketed the
knife and decided not to respond. Then she made another decision. She stalked across the quarry to the holding pen, dependents scrambling out of her path.

It wasn't locked.

THEY WILL NOT AWAKEN YOU HAVE NO ALLIES NO HOPE
FOR AID

"I have a pretty good idea that you've done just about
all to me you're willing to risk if we're going to be, what
was it? *Integrated?*" Marcia stepped over a slumbering soldier. It was the captain. His eyes were moving back and
forth rapidly behind closed lids.

At the center of the pen, she picked up the first pistol
she found, considered it briefly, then tossed it to one side.
There had to be something here she could use.

THERE IS NOTHING THERE YOU CAN USE

Again . . . As with the captain's talk of war stories, *again*
someone—or some*thing*—answered her with words

she'd only thought, never spoken.

As with the captain . . .

"Why me?" asked Marcia, damning her cloudy head, thinking hard.

OF THE SIXTY-FIVE POSSIBLE CANDIDATES YOU ARE THE MOST SUITABLE YOU ARE TWICE THE AGE OF THE NEXT ELDEST

The Commodore's voice had modulated somewhat. It sounded . . . pleased.

"You want me over all these soldiers because I'm *older* than them? Shouldn't you choose someone with a strong body?" She didn't stop pawing through the mound of gear.

THE BATHYSPHERE IS THE MOST SOPHISTICATED LIFE-SUPPORT MECHANISM EVER DEVISED AMANDEEP KIRMANI WAS SEVENTY-ONE YEARS OLD WHEN WE INTEGRATED HIS FLESH LIVED AND THRIVED THROUGHOUT THE REIGN OF ATHENA PARTHENUS AND SURVIVED FOR ALMOST THREE YEARS AFTER WE CRASHED INTO THIS HILLSIDE

"And then what happened? You shut down?" She found several cube-shaped green boxes, metallic and dangerous-looking, plastered with warning labels and brightly colored graphics. These had been stacked much more carefully than the rest of the gear. The word "explosive" figured prominently in the warnings.

UNTIL THE SERVITORS ARRIVED AND INITIATED A

LIMITED REBOOT YES

Marcia considered that. There was so much here she didn't understand.

"Why not take one of the dependents to be your, what, pilot?" She looked through the fence. The silo hand was watching her, and she gestured at them. "Take that one. They've got a lot on the ball." *And are clearly up to something . . .*

THE PHYSIOLOGICAL PROFILES OF THE SERVITORS PRECLUDE INTEGRATION THE BATHYSPHERE AND THE PROTOCOLS WERE DESIGNED FOR HUMANS THE MONOTISSUES OF THE SERVITORS WOULD WREAK HAVOC WITH MY SYSTEMS

And there it was. That was why she kept thinking about the captain. It wasn't his humanity. It wasn't what he had said about the impossibility of restoring humanity to a Commodore.

"I have a proposal for you," Marcia said. She picked up two of the cubes. They were lighter than she'd thought they would be. The instructions printed on their labels were distressingly simple.

ISSUE IT THOUGH YOU LACK BARGAINING POSITION IF YOU WILL NOT INTEGRATE BY CHOICE OTHER PROTOCOLS ARE AVAILABLE TO ME

Marcia set one of the cubes down among the sprawled bodies of the soldiers, broke a plastic seal, and twisted a dial. She carried the other one outside the pen and looked up at the Commodore's physical structure. It was almost free.

"I'm going to offer you two options," she said. "One is that you choose an alternate of my choice from among these soldiers to take onboard."

I HAVE CHOSEN YOU

"Option two is that I let that charge pod explode and kill all of them and let this second one explode and kill me—and probably damage you quite a bit—and then you're back where you started."

For once, the Commodore didn't answer immediately. A half dozen heartbeats—*fast* heartbeats, admittedly—passed. Then it said, I CALCULATE THAT YOU WILL NOT CARRY OUT YOUR THREAT TO TERMINATE THE OTHER HUMANS

Shit.

BUT THERE IS A SIGNIFICANT PROBABILITY THAT YOU WILL ATTEMPT TO DAMAGE MY CHASSIS AND END YOUR OWN LIFE

Another few heartbeats.

THEREFORE I AGREE TO YOUR PROPOSAL

———

Marcia didn't drag the captain up and into the black sphere near the center of the Commodore's body mass.

The silo hand did.

And they did so with alacrity.

As they climbed, Marcia turned the captain's words over in her head. *I will kill anyone. I will die. I will not fail.*

I'm hardly anyone at all.

"Careful of his head, there," said Marcia. They had picked up the captain and flung him over their shoulder as soon as Brother Fortran had made his pronouncement. The captain's head hung to the silo hand's heels, and every time the dependent made a turn on the zig-zag route upward, Marcia was afraid the man's skull was going to be cracked open on a rock or a pylon or some protruding bit of the Commodore itself.

Why am I worried about him, though? This is what he wanted.

Was it? And would the preponderance of monotissues in the man's body somehow allow him to take control of the Commodore instead of the other way around?

It was a thin theory.

It was what she had.

Her goals now were the escape of the soldiers and the elimination of the threat posed by the Commodore. Brother Fortran had not made its own goals clear beyond "integration" but Marcia was well aware of what a functioning war machine of the Voluntary State was capable of. She would have been aware of it even without the captain's reminder.

She told herself, again, that the captain would approve of her plan, had he been conscious to know of it. She kept thinking that over and over again.

There was little in the way of ceremony or preparation once they'd reached the bathysphere. A crack appeared along its vertical length, and when this had opened wide enough, the silo hand dumped the captain inside, then immediately turned and started back down. They waved at Marcia impatiently when she didn't follow right away.

INTEGRATION IMMINENT said Brother Fortran. Now the machine's voice was flatter, devoid of expression.

Marcia felt a tug at her pants leg. The silo hand had reached up from the scaffolding ladder. There was a rushing sound as gravel began pouring down from above, dislodged by the vibration she was just now noticing.

"Oh, hell," she said, and began frantically climbing down.

She was sure the Commodore was about to stand and then take devastating action before leaping into the sky. Instead, the vibration subsided.

"Hello?" said Marcia.

"Hello!" said the silo hand.

They didn't immediately say anything further, because a knot of other dependents crowded in, hooting and whistling. The silo hand listened to all this, then pointed

toward the pen. If they made any comprehensible vo-
calizations, Marcia didn't hear them. Nonetheless, the
whole cove was suddenly alive with dependents running
in every direction, too many to track.

Since she couldn't follow them all with her eyes, Marcia watched those lugging explosives up to the quarry
top.

"You're killing it *now*? Why did you help it before
then? Why did you dig it up?"

"Not killing," said the silo hand. "*Hiding.*"

"Hiding from who?"

The silo hand pointed at the pen, where the soldiers
still hadn't stirred.

"So, they'll wake up, then?"

"Maybe!"

Then they shoved her, and she went to the ground
just as a blast sounded from above. Boulders and rocks
and loose earth spilled out and down from the top of the
quarry's workface. Marcia choked on the dust cloud.

The Commodore was completely hidden.

When she regained her feet, she saw that the silo hand
was looking over at the soldiers. Still no motion there.
They shrugged again. "Maybe not!"

The first of what she saw was a long line of dependents walking by. They were all bent under bundles of
various kinds, including some colored the olive drab

of the federal soldiery, yes, but also some in colors and materials Marcia recognized from other contexts. The rough weave of burlap from the grange. The yellow and black stripes of heavy equipment hauling.

"Where are you going?" Marcia asked, as it became apparent the whole cove was emptying out.

The silo hand shook their head, though whether that meant they didn't know or weren't willing to say, Marcia couldn't decide.

"How did you coordinate all this? There are dependents from all over the Commonwealth here, aren't there?"

A little harvester came up, burdened with two packs. One of these was set down before the silo hand, then the harvester hustled back to its place in the slow-moving line.

As they shrugged on the pack, the silo hand said, "We are not dependents. We are *in*dependents."

FINALLY

It was long after sunset when the soldiers began stirring. Marcia had decided to give them until morning before heading back to town on her own for help. She was confident the county sheriff would offer her aid. Then, as the two platoons began rousing, she heard a voice, doubly familiar, doubly unfamiliar.

"*I have something to teach you.*" It was coming from nowhere and everywhere.

"You survived," said Marcia.

"*No,*" said the voice.

"Then how are you communicating with me?"

There was a reply, but not an answer.

> "*Servitor lurking,*
> *All the while working.*"

A mnemonic.

"Is that your name now? Servitor?" She was whispering.

"Agent!" The shout was from the pen. "Agent, where is the captain?" It was Sergeant Moss's voice.

She waited a moment before heading for the enclosure. There was no answer to her question. There was no answer to the sergeant's question, either.

About the Author

© 2022 Gwenda Bond

CHRISTOPHER ROWE is the author of the acclaimed story collection *Telling the Map,* as well as a middle-grade series the Supernormal Sleuthing Service cowritten with his wife, author Gwenda Bond. He has been a finalist for the Hugo, Nebula, World Fantasy, Neukom, and Theodore Sturgeon Awards. He lives in a hundred-year-old house in Lexington, Kentucky, with his wife and their many unruly pets.

TOR·COM

Science fiction. Fantasy. The universe.

And related subjects.

*

More than just a publisher's website, *Tor.com*
is a venue for **original fiction, comics,** and
discussion of the entire field of SF and fantasy,
in all media and from all sources. Visit our site
today—and join the conversation yourself.